Ronnie
and
Rosey

Bradbury Press ∞ Scarsdale, New York

Ronnie
and
Rosey

by Judie Angell

1 2 3 4 5   81 80 79 78 77
The text of this book is set in 12 pt. Janson.

Library of Congress Cataloging in Publication Data
Angell, Judie. Ronnie and Rosey.
Summary: Just when things are looking up for thirteen-year-old Ronnie, her father dies, creating a void she and her mother have trouble filling.
[1. Death—Fiction.   2. Friendship—Fiction]
I. Title.
PZ7.A5824Ro   [Fic]   77-75362
ISBN 0-87888-124-7

For My Parents
with love

Ronnie
and
Rosey

Straight Man

Chapter 1

You know what's weird? Something will happen to you . . . some little nothing thing you don't think about at the time. But much later on, you find that everything started with that one little nothing thing.

I mean, it almost makes you wonder about Fate, or about somebody pulling the strings on you like you were a puppet, just making things happen to you. Pulling you here, pushing you there, and you really have no control over it at all.

Like the funny ways you meet people who turn out to be terribly important to you.

When we moved to Uniondale last year, I was thirteen. And so scared of my new school—Benjamin Franklin Junior High. It was absolutely huge.

But the first week, I met Robert.

∞

"OW! Hey, watch where you're going!" I yelled. I looked down at the floor and saw my books being scattered.

"Oh, boy, I'm sorry," this boy said, trying to collect everything, mine and his.

"Forget it, just go get my math homework, okay?" I pointed. "Some kid is skating down the hall on it."

"Right, right," and he hustled over there. "Hey, I'm really sorry," he said, handing the paper to me. "Man, this is only the first week of school and I'm starting already!"

"Starting what?" I asked, putting my stuff together.

"You're the second person I zonked into today."

I started to laugh. "It might've been my fault. I'm new here and I'm still looking for my classrooms."

"Well, at least I didn't knock you down. The person I rammed yesterday was my Spanish teacher."

"She went down?"

"Like a pail of sand balancing on a pencil point. What's your name?"

"Ronnie."

"Short for Veronica?" he asked.

"Short for nothing. What's yours?"

"Robert."

"Well, thanks for picking up my stuff, Robert. See ya." He waved and I made it to Gym before the bell.

It was Thursday, but only the second day of school. Labor Day was Monday, and Tuesday, I guess, was recuperation from Monday, so they started school Wednesday. I had already been to all of my classes except Music, so I had just one more roll call to get through. There's this thing about my name. Everybody thinks it's a boy's.

I was really named after my grandmother, whose name was Ronah, but my parents hated that and instead just gave me her nickname. In my old school, in Lynbrook, everybody was used to it, but at Franklin I had to start all over.

I'd had Gym the day before, so I figured the attendance call would go smoothly. I changed into my uniform—purple track shorts and white top, just like the boys', and went into the gym and sat on the floor with the rest of the class. There is supposed to be a law about girls having to have gym with the boys but this school hadn't gotten around to doing anything about it. There was a big folding screenlike thing that they kept closed, separating the boys' gym from the girls'. It didn't bother me too much, but my mother sort of supported Women's Lib and she'd muttered about their getting with it when I told her.

The Gym teacher, Miss Fisk, was moving toward my end of the alphabet.

"Rabin, Joan?"

"Here."

"Racanelli, Evelyn?"

"Here."

"Rachman, Ronald? Oh, I'm sorry, I haven't changed that yet."

Terrific.

She stopped and made a correction with a red pencil she pulled out of her sweat sock. "Rachman, Ronnie?"

"Right," I said. Miss Fisk didn't look at all like some people picture lady Gym teachers. I mean, I once heard my Uncle Fred kidding about women who teach Phys. Ed. He said you couldn't tell them from the men, that they had big shoulders and muscles and wore thick sweat socks and smoked cigars. Boy, my mom really went at him over that, said it was terrible to stereotype people. So I figured when Mom got a load of Miss Fisk, she'd invite her over for dinner just to meet Uncle Fred and watch his theory go out the window. Miss Fisk was gorgeous. If she had muscles, they sure were in all the right places. And she had beautiful skin, somewhere between black and coffee-colored, and a kind of moderate-Afro hairdo that just kind of framed her face. She *did* have on thick sweat socks, but you could tell she had great legs.

"Okay, girls," Miss Fisk was saying, "today we're going to start with calisthenics and then we'll try some rope climbing."

The girl next to me groaned. I looked at her and could tell right away why she was groaning. She must've weighed about three times as much as I did.

We stood up and spread out in rows. The heavy girl moved to the back and I followed.

Miss Fisk blew her whistle. "Left hand on hip, right hand up over the head! Ready, bend, bend, *bend!*"

"Cow patties!" the fat girl said.

"What?" I asked, as we bent, bent, *bent.*

"I said 'cow patties'. I don't like to swear in front of people I don't know."

"*Other hand!*" Miss Fisk yelled and we had to bend the other way.

"Listen, feel free," I said. "I hate this, too."

"You'd hate it more if you were me," the girl said.

"Guess I would."

"*Touch your toes!*" from Fisk.

"No way," the girl grunted. "I can't get past my knees. I can't even *see* my knees!"

"*Jumping Jacks!*" Fisk yelled, and the sound of hands clapping in rhythm echoed in the gym.

"*Relax!*" was the next command, and we all sat down.

"What's your name?" I asked.

"Evelyn. I know yours . . . I'm in your French class."

"Oh." I thought rope climbing must be as big a drag for her as being called Ronald is for me. "Why don't you go to the girls' room during rope climbing?"

Evelyn twisted her lips and shook her head. "Fisk is onto that. I did that all last year. Are you new here?"

"Let's line up in front of the ropes!"

"Oh, boy, here we go," Evelyn said, and edged slowly backward.

"Yeah, I just moved from Lynbrook three weeks ago," I told her. "Big school isn't it?"

"Well, that's because they're busing a lot of us here from Uniondale."

"Oh, I know. I live in Uniondale, too," I said.

"No kidding? What street?"

"Walnut."

"You're in the tree-streets, too? Great!" Evelyn said.

"The what?"

"Tree-streets. There are about five blocks . . . just a minute." Evelyn looked behind her down the line of kids. "Come with me." She left the line again to move backwards. "Maggie, let me get in back of you," she said to a girl near the center, and pulled me in front of her. "See, she'll notice me if I get at the very end of the line," Evelyn explained, "but if I just keep sneaking around in the middle, sometimes I never get to the front . . ." I laughed. "Well, anyway, there are about five blocks in Uniondale named after trees. I'm on one of them, too—Spruce. We live just three blocks from each other."

"You know anything about the Uniondale school?"

"Like what? I know it was supposed to be finished this September."

"Well, is it going to be a combination junior high and high school like this one?" I asked.

"Yeah, but much smaller. It'll be nicer when we get over there. You'll see."

"Evelyn, do we have any classes together besides French?" Evelyn was the first person I'd really spoken to since school started and I liked her.

"Let's check our schedule cards when we get to the showers. Oh, jeez, we're getting closer to the front. What time is it?"

"Five after 1:00," I told her. "How much time for showers, ten minutes?"

"Yeah. Twelve minutes left in the gym. I'll never make it. What if I faint?"

"Did you do that last year?" I asked.

"No. Never tried that one."

I shrugged. "Well, okay, go ahead."

But she hung back. "I think I'll wait till the very last minute to use up more time," she said, and we moved to the end of the line. Miss Fisk had not even looked our way.

"How about taking the bus home together?" Evelyn asked. "They run about every ten minutes when school lets out. Why don't I meet you across the street from Harry's Luncheonette?"

"Sure, fine," I answered. "Right after the last bell. Uh oh, we're here."

"Hi, Evelyn." Miss Fisk smiled. "No more girls left to sneak in back of, eh?"

Evelyn looked at me and rolled her eyes.

"Let's go, hon," Fisk said.

"I feel dizzy," Evelyn mumbled, swaying a bit. I had been about to climb my rope, but stopped and began to look worried to help her out.

Miss Fisk didn't look at all worried. "Evelyn Racanelli, if you think I'm buying that old trick . . ."

"No, no . . . I really don't feel well," Evelyn said. "I have to sit down." And she did.

I started to climb my rope, but it was hard, trying to catch Evelyn's act on the ground while aiming my body for the ceiling.

"I mean it," Evelyn said with her head down. "Feel how cold my hands are."

I watched her hold up a limp wrist, while I was trying to inch my way up the rope. First I'd jump with my feet, then grab the rope with my knees. It hurt.

"Your hands are cold because you're nervous, Evelyn. Come on, I'll help you," Fisk tried to help Evelyn up but it was a lost cause, so she just looked down at the heap on the floor and shook her head.

"Okay, okay," the Gym teacher said, "but I can't let you get away with this again."

Evelyn nodded weakly.

"That's a promise, Evelyn," Fisk said, and turned back to the ropes.

∞

"Evelyn, I think I really believed you," I told her on the way to the shower. "You turned white and everything!"

"Wasn't that good?" she asked, grinning. "I just think about Sara Lee going out of business and I turn white!" I laughed. "I'm going to be an actress some day," she said seriously.

"No kidding?"

She nodded. "Oh, yes. In fact, I've already started."

"How?"

"My friend and I got up an act we're going to do for the Methodist Church fall fund-raiser. They're having a variety show. They have one every year but it's usually awful. Same old stuff. Bonnie Beardsley twirls her fire baton and Mrs. Nagerney sings *Alice Blue Gown!*"

"Sounds terrific," I said.

"This year it's going to be different. Partly because we're doing an act," Evelyn said, smiling, "but also because Bonnie Beardsley moved away and Mrs. Nagerney had a fight with Mrs. Farber and they're not talking."

"Who's Mrs. Farber?"

"She runs the show."

"Oh."

After the shower, which I took and she didn't—*"Nobody* sees me in my ever-lovin'," she said—Evelyn and I checked our schedules. We found we had Home Room, French, Lunch, Gym and Music together. Well, Gym and Music alternated, with Gym on Monday, Wednesday and Thursday, and Music on Tuesday and Friday.

It wasn't easy juggling schedules and books and stuff in the halls. There were so many kids traveling from class to class whenever there was a bell I felt like a piece of Lego jammed into a toy house.

I edged her over against the wall so the flow of traffic could keep flowing. "With so many kids at Franklin, how come we have all these classes together?" I asked.

"The alphabet," she answered. "Racanelli, Rachman. It's easier to organize classes alphabetically. We're not people, we're just numbers and letters to that Great School System in the Sky. Listen, next year it'll be different when our own school is built. I gotta go. See you on the corner after ninth period!"

That's how I met Evelyn. Robert and Evelyn in the same day. And only the second day of school, too. Even Miss Fisk . . . three people who went through it all with me. All of us, so close . . .

Evelyn and I *did* take the bus home together and she showed me the rows of tree-named streets as we walked from the corner. They were all together, she said. Other streets were named in clumps like that, too. There was the fruit-street clump: Peach Street, Pear Street, etc. And there was also a clump of President-streets: Coolidge, Roosevelt, Harding. Evelyn said it made it easy to tell what side of town anyone lived on.

"It's another kind of lumping people together for convenience," she said. "Like throwing us in classes by alphabet. The science-fiction writers weren't far from wrong, you know. We're being controlled by outside forces."

"You really think so?"

"Well, right now, they're mostly human. But in another few years? All computers. And robots. Wanna come in for a snack?"

We had reached her house on Spruce Street.

"Oh, thanks, but I gotta get home. We're still unpacking. We've been in this house three weeks and the most we've dug out is changes of underwear."

"That's all?"

"Just about. See, it's only the three of us, Mom, Dad and me, and we live ultra-casual. I guess Mom's always been like that, but I wish I knew which carton my left shoe was in."

"I bet." Evelyn smiled. "Does your father work in the city?"

"Yeah, does yours?"

"Uh huh. He takes the 7:52 in the morning."

"Mine, too. Do you have brothers or sisters?"

"Two great big brothers," Evelyn sighed. "It's a losing race to the refrigerator when they're around."

I looked at her and she laughed.

"I know, I know" she said. "I don't look like I lose too often. But they're not always around!"

"Did you ever try dieting?" I asked and bit my tongue.

But Evelyn didn't seem to mind. "You know, I did, once. But it is absolutely no fun. I'd much rather eat than diet. See you tomorrow on the bus!" She waved and I continued my three-block walk home.

Mom was in her studio when I got there. Actually, it was the third bedroom in our house, but since we didn't have another kid, Mom and Dad set it up as a painting studio.

"Hi, babe," Mom called.

I waded through the boxes in the living room, past the cartons in the hall, and between the crates in the studio. "Hi," I said.

"Nice day?"

"Yeah." I kissed her on the top of her head and peered over her shoulder at the canvas. She reached around to give me a hug.

I shrieked. "You got paint on one-half of my skirt wardrobe!"

She laughed. "Are you kidding? You mean you only have two skirts unpacked?"

"Yeah! How many do *you* have?"

"None!" and we both cracked up.

"Hey, I met a really neat girl at school today. She only lives three blocks from here . . . What are those blue triangles?"

" 'The Essence of Dreams'. What's her name?" Mom picked up her brush again.

"Evelyn Racanelli. What do you mean, 'The Essence of Dreams'?"

"I don't really know," Mom answered. "But doesn't it sound terrific?" She dabbed some red paint on an orange circle that divided the blue triangles.

"Her father takes the same train to the city as Daddy. Are you gonna be finished soon? We've *got* to get some of this stuff out of the way."

"Honey, you're right. You're absolutely right!" She started to laugh. "First thing tomorrow morning!"

"Mom . . . ?" I said, making a grab for her paint brush, which she pulled out of my reach.

"I'm kidding, just kidding," she said, picking up a palette knife and smearing the orange triangle.

"Listen, Ronnie, why don't you start on the stuff in your room? I'll help out, I promise, just as soon as I get this thing to look like what I had in mind. Okay?"

I went into my room and looked over the boxes.

"It's all labeled, Ronnie," Mom called.

"Well, yeah, but it's labeled *wrong!*" I yelled back. "The box marked SWEATERS—RONNIE turned out to be summer and winter pajamas!"

"How did that happen?" Mom yelled.

I called back, "Either we put the wrong label on the box, or we put the wrong stuff in the box with the right label!"

"I'll be right there," from Mom.

I sorted out two cartons and Mom still hadn't come in.

"Hey, Mom," I yelled. "Aren't you finished yet?"

"Sorry, honey, I just had to get that last bit. How 'bout a break. Did you have a snack yet?"

"Not yet, but . . . oh, okay, let's get something."

I made Mom laugh when I told her about Evelyn in Gym class. I didn't mention Robert knocking down my books. I had forgotten about him . . .

Dad came just as Mom was finishing her coffee.

"Boy, you girls must be exhausted from all that work!" he said, kissing Mom and then me. We looked at him and laughed. "What a difference in the living room from when I left this morning!"

"Oh, well," I began, "we haven't started the *living* room yet . . ."

"Ronnie's been working on her *own* room," Mom said. "There's a *big* difference there, right, Ronnie?"

"Big!" I said.

"Well," Daddy said, "I came home from the office early to get a lot done here, so let's get to it, okay, Dottie? Ready, Ron?"

"Dear, you just got here," Mom said. "Wouldn't you like a cup of coffee first?"

"Ah, well . . . okay," Daddy said, pulling up a chair. "Why don't you tell me how you both spent your day."

Most of our unpacking times went like that.

∞

Around 5:00, Dad said, "Let's go to Mc-Donald's."

"Aww, Kentucky Fried," I said.

Mom and Dad both groaned. "Hamburgers," Dad said.

"Chicken," I insisted.

Mom said, "All right, let's toss for it. Who's got a coin?"

Daddy had the coin. "What'll it be? One-time-only or two-out-of-three?"

"Two-out-of-three!" I said.

"Call it!" Dad said as he tossed the coin in the air and made it land on the back of his hand.

"Heads!" I yelled.

"Heads!" he said and smiled.

"Okay," I said, "One-time-only!"

"Aw no," Mom laughed, "can't do that. You said two-out-of-three."

The next two tosses came up tails.

"Burgers!" they both said together.
But Daddy drove to Kentucky Fried Chicken.

Chapter 2

Evelyn and I had lunch together fifth period the next day. Since we had only about forty minutes for lunch, forty-three to be exact, Evelyn said we should get moving as soon as fourth period was over. We rushed to the corner across the street from Harry's.

There were two luncheonettes opposite the school. Harry's was on one corner and Blue Dell's was on the other.

"How come we're going to a luncheonette?" I asked Evelyn as we crossed the street. "Looks like we'll never get through the door."

Evelyn was already opening her lunchbag. "Doesn't matter," she said, poking around in the bag. "We have our food already."

"Well then, why bother? Why don't we just find some place to sit down?"

"No, Ronnie, you're supposed to stand outside Harry's and lean up against the wall to eat."

"Why?"

"Because that's how you keep in touch with the world. I mean, Harry's Luncheonette is the gossip center of the universe. You hear *everything* there. You were in junior high last year. Where did you have lunch?"

"Oh, in Lynbrook we ate in the cafeteria. The nearest luncheonette was five blocks away."

"Yeah, we'll have the same thing next year in ninth grade. But now, with so many kids, this is the only place to talk . . . Okay, now we have a good piece of wall to lean on and we can still be sort of half inside and hear what's going on."

"Hey, Betty, you kicked me in the ankle!" one girl yelled.

"I did not, I'm over here!" another screamed back.

"Well, who was that then?"

"Hi, Racanelli!" a boy called, punching Evelyn on the arm. She punched him back without answering. She was starting on the biggest ham-cheese-tomato-bacon sandwich I had ever seen.

Someone from inside screeched, *"Watch it!* I just dropped my glasses!"

A girl's voice: "Where?"

"Under your shoe, you idiot!"

"Evelyn," I said, "what is so terrific about over-hearing this world-shaking stuff?"

"Because," she answered, pausing before another bite, "sometimes you get neat little tidbits. You have to keep your ears open. And by the way, don't ever go to Blue Dell's down the street."

"How come?"

"Because the kids that hang out there aren't the ones you want to know. Ask me why not while I take another bite."

"Why not?"

She held up her hand, meaning wait a minute. She had to chew more.

"Peanut butter!" someone yelled in my ear. But he wasn't talking to me.

"Again?" someone yelled in my other ear. "You *always* bring peanut butter!"

Evelyn said, "Gloria, you just shattered my friend's eardrum. Would you please move over here?" Gloria moved. "Now listen, Ronnie," she continued, "I'm about to further your education. Blue Dell's is a hang-out, that's where they deal dope. It's always getting raided, so just stay away from there. Hey, is that all you brought? A cup of yogurt? I kept waiting for you to take out more lunch."

"No, that's all I brought. Why?"

"How can you get through the day on just that?"

"That's all . . ."

"Shh!" Evelyn said quickly and leaned way over to her right. "Did you hear that?"

"Hear what? How can you hear anyth—"

"Shh!" Back to the right again. Then she stood up and leaned in toward me. "Cindy Citrenbaum just said that she heard from Karen Farber that Miss Fisk is going out with Mr. Vincent."

"Miss Fisk, the Gym teacher?" I asked.

"Yeah. I told you you can hear everything here. You just have to keep your ears open and pick up on the right things."

"Well, how do you know if it's true?"

Evelyn shook her head at me. "I just *told* you! Cindy Citrenbaum heard it from Karen Farber."

"But . . ."

"Karen Farber knows everything. Just keep your ears open." I did, but nothing came through on my line. Finally it was time to go back in.

"We have Music eighth period," Evelyn called as we separated. "See you then!" And she disappeared into the crowd.

∞

I had Science sixth period and Social Studies after that with Mr. Vincent. I looked at him more carefully than I had the other two days. He didn't stand out in my mind because he misread my name the first day like everybody else. The only people I remember are the ones that get it right the first time. And I think there are only two of those, both related to me.

Mr. Vincent wasn't bad looking. A little old—I guess in his thirties. No wedding ring. So what if he was dating Miss Fisk? *She* wasn't married, either. Oh, probably they were uptight because she's black and he's white. People get uptight over such dumb stuff.

Music was next. I thought, *the last time I'll be called "Ronald" until we have a substitute.*

"Hey, Ronnie!"

I turned around. Evelyn was standing at her locker with the boy who accidentally dumped my books the day before.

"Ronnie, meet my oldest friend, Robert Rose."

"Yeah, we, uh, ran into each other already," I said. "Hi again."

"Hi, Ron."

"Robert and I grew up together," Evelyn said. "He lives on Chestnut Street, a tree-street buddy."

"Oh."

Evelyn looked at me. "What do you mean, you ran into each other yesterday?"

"What do you *think* she means?" Robert asked.

"That's what I *thought* she meant," Evelyn said.

"What are you talking about?" I asked.

"See, I've known him a long time," Evelyn explained, as we walked into the Music Room and took seats. "Robert is either walking into walls—or people—or he's getting in trouble. Usually for something he didn't do, but mostly for something he did."

"But nothing bad," Robert said. "Just dumb. Like the whole class could be talking, flying paper airplanes or passing notes, and *I* will be the one who gets yelled at for turning around in my seat. It's like there's this enormous rain cloud that sits right over my head."

"I think I see it," I said.

"But we all forgive him because he plays terrific

piano. Wait'll you hear him," Evelyn said. "He's the one I'm doing the act with."

"The one you were telling me about? For the Methodist Church?" I asked.

"Right! Wait'll you see it." Evelyn said.

"I'd like that," I said as the bell rang.

∞

The three of us took the bus home together after school. We all had to stand because the bus was mobbed.

"Whaddya wanna do this weekend, Ev?" Robert asked. "Should we go to a movie?"

"No, let's have a party!" Evelyn said. "We can invite the kids in the neighborhood so Ronnie can meet them."

"It'll have to be at your place," Robert said, lurching to one side as the bus turned a corner. "My father's going to be home all weekend."

Evelyn turned to me. "Robert and his father don't get along," she explained.

"You don't get along with him, either," Robert said.

"And neither do his two sisters or his mother," Evelyn said and they both laughed. "Sure, we can have it at my house. Okay, Ronnie?"

"Oh . . . Yeah," I said.

"Who can we ask?" Robert wanted to know.

"Well, Bev and Diane, and Barbara, and Helen . . . and Skunky . . ."

"Skunky?"

"He has eight cats," Robert told me, "and he always smells like kitty litter."

"Sounds like fun . . ." I said.

"How about Billy Fenner?" Robert asked.

"He won't come," Evelyn said.

"Yes, he will," Robert said, "he likes those cheese puff things you make. Hey, here's our stop."

We fought our way off the bus, with Evelyn as buffer.

"All right, party time Saturday night. Right?" Robert said as we began to walk toward the tree-streets.

"I'll have to ask," I told him, "but I'm sure it'll be okay."

"Call me tonight," Evelyn said when we reached her street, "and let me know. Then I'll call every-body else."

∞

"Can I go to a party tomorrow night?" I asked at dinner.

"Where?" Dad wanted to know.

I told them and how I couldn't pass up this great opportunity to meet somebody named "Skunky."

Mom said, "Would you rather do that than go to a movie with us?"

"Sure she would," Daddy said, "but we'd better stay home ourselves if she's going to be out."

"Why, Daddy? You guys go out. I'll only be a couple of blocks away. And if you go to an early show, you'll be home before I will."

They agreed and I went to call Evelyn.

"What should I wear?" I asked her.

"Oh, just jeans," she answered. "Listen, what can you cook for the party?"

"I can only make scrambled eggs," I told her.

She laughed. "You can't stick a toothpick in scrambled eggs."

"You can the way I make them," I answered.

"Forget it, just bring a bag of pretzels. I have everything else. See you tomorrow about 8:00!"

Chapter 3

"Hi, Ronnie, come on in! Everybody's here!"

Evelyn met me at the door holding a tray full of weird-looking brown things. I stepped into her living room.

"Have a cheese puff," she said.

"Wait'll I take off my jacket."

"Hey, let's have one of those, Evelyn," a tall boy said, picking up one of the brown things.

"Ronnie, this is Billy Fenner. He lives next door to Robert on Chestnut."

"Hi," I said.

"Hi," Billy answered.

"Who's playing the piano?" I asked, noticing the music for the first time. "Is that Robert?"

"Yup," Evelyn said, "I told you he was good. He takes lessons, but he's better than his teacher. He plays by ear, he doesn't need music. His teacher's trying to teach him to read the notes, but she's losing the battle. He just takes off on his own."

I started to walk over to the piano, but Evelyn put down the tray and took my arm.

"Just let me introduce you around," she said. "Then you can go watch Robert. He'll love it—a new audience."

We moved over to a group of girls in a corner of the living room.

"Bev, Barbara, Helen . . . this is Ronnie. She just moved to Walnut."

They all said "Hi."

"Are you in eighth, too?" the girl named Bev asked. I nodded.

"Oh, nice," Barbara said.

And then the conversation died.

"I, uh, just moved from Lynbrook," I offered.

"Oh, I used to know someone from there," Helen said. "Do you know Carl Sills?"

"Um, no I don't."

"Oh."

Another pause.

Then both Helen and Bev started talking at once and laughed.

"You first."

"No, you."

"Well," Bev said, "I was just wondering if you had heard about the 'Y'. I mean, did you join or anything?"

"No," I said, "I haven't heard about it. You mean the YMCA?"

"Yeah," Helen said, "there's one in town, near the school. They have neat parties and Mr. Vincent runs the kids' program. He's really nice."

"Mr. Vincent, the Social Studies teacher?" I asked. "The one who's . . ."

"The one who's what?"

"Nothing. I must have been thinking of someone else."

"No, that's him," Bev said, "he's the Soc. teacher. He runs a great program down there. And you should see him in jeans!" The girls smiled at each other.

"You should join, Ronnie. It's a lot of fun. Right, Evelyn?"

Evelyn was back with another tray. This one had paper cups filled with Coke on it. We all took one.

"Join what?" Evelyn asked.

"The 'Y'," Helen said. "We were just telling Ronnie about the program."

"Oh, yeah, it's good, Ronnie. We'll take you down there sometime."

"Great," I said, and sipped my Coke. "Listen, where's Skunky?" I *had* to see what a "Skunky" looked like.

"Gee, I don't know," Evelyn said, looking around, "*Skunk!*"

"*Yeah!*" from the kitchen.

"*C'mere!*"

A boy with hair in his eyes like a sheepdog's appeared from the kitchen.

"Skunk, this is Ronnie New Girl. She's been dying to meet you."

"She has?"

I jabbed Evelyn. "Hi, uh, Skunky."

"Hi, Ronnie."

"Evelyn says you like cats," I said.

"Oh, I *love* 'em. You like cats?"

"Well, I never knew any personally."

"Oh, well, you don't know what you're missing."

He looked like he was about to give me a long history of the species *cat*, so I quickly said, "Gee, I've never heard Robert play before. I'd like to go over and listen awhile. Want to come?"

Skunky backed toward the kitchen again. "No, thanks, I've heard him. Besides, I'm keeping an eye on the next batch of cheese puffs. See, if you don't watch them carefully while they're baking, they shrivel."

"Shrivel?"

"Yeah, they come out looking like little raisins."

I walked over to the piano. ''You are really good!'' I said.

He looked up and smiled. "Hi, Ron. Thanks."

"I know that song," I said, leaning over the top of the baby grand. "It's from 'Chorus Line'. My parents took me to see it last year."

"You *saw* it? Boy, you're lucky. I'd give anything to see it." He didn't even look at the keys while he was talking to me, and he went right into another song.

"*As Time Goes By!*" I cried.

"How do *you* know that song?" Robert asked without missing a beat.

"I know *every* song," I said, smiling. "Anyway, that one's from an old movie, 'Casablanca'. My mother watches it every time it's on TV. But I do have a good memory for music. And words. Sometimes when I'm feeling bad I think of a song to fit my mood and it makes me feel better."

"Hey, me, too!" he said.

"Are you going to play piano in the act you're doing with Evelyn?" I asked.

"Oh, sure, that's what I do," he said. "Evelyn's the actress."

"What kind of act is it?"

"She's going to pantomime a girl buying a bathing suit. Y'know, she goes into the store, points to what she wants and it's four sizes smaller than what she needs. Then she pantomimes trying it on, wiggling into it—you know."

"It sounds funny," I said.

"Well, it ought to be. *She's* funny, but, I don't know. It's not right yet."

"I'd really like to see it."

"Hey, Rosey!" It was Billy Fenner. "Play something fast, man!"

Robert curled his lip.

"Rosey?" I asked. "Is that your nickname?"

"Unfortunately," Robert answered. "Funny,

isn't it? You have the boy's name and I've got the girl's."

I didn't know what to say to that, so I looked away from the piano as he began playing *The Hustle*. Billy Fenner started to dance.

He wasn't very good, but he was energetic. A new girl had appeared from somewhere and was sitting on the couch with Bev, Helen and Barbara. Evelyn was standing in the middle of the room looking around.

"This is a dead party!" she yelled suddenly. "It needs some pizzazz! Somebody think of something."

"How about singing Christmas carols?" Robert asked from the piano. Evelyn ignored him.

"How about 'Post Office'?" from Billy Fenner.

"Blagh," from Barbara, Helen, Bev and the new girl.

"Charades?" Skunky said, re-appearing from the kitchen.

"*I* know!" An evil gleam shone in Evelyn's eyes as she smiled.

"What?" we all said at once.

"Let's play with my brother's C.B.!"

Cries of "Oh, terrific!"; "Can we?"; "Oh, boy!"

"He won't be back for hours!" Evelyn said. "And he's got a base, right in his room on this floor."

"Lenny will kill you, Evelyn," Robert warned.

"Lenny will never know!" Evelyn said.

"Well, what'll we say?" asked the girl whose name I didn't know.

"That's what we'll have to figure out," Evelyn said, pulling a footstool over to the couch. "We'll have to do a whole act and plan it all out. Beverly, think of something."

"You're the actress, Evelyn," Bev said. "You think of something."

"Gee, I haven't met you," the new girl said to me.

"Oh, gosh, I'm sorry," Evelyn said. "I didn't know you hadn't met. Ronnie, this is Diane. Elm."

"Diane Elm?"

Diane laughed. "No, Diane *Hetrick*. I *live* on Elm."

"Hi, Diane."

"Hi, Ronnie."

"Enough small talk!" Evelyn said. "Think! We need a script."

"You mean you want to act out a *play* on the C.B.?" Billy Fenner asked.

"Kind of," Evelyn said, "but we can only plan our own lines. We can't account for what the other person will answer."

"*I* have an idea," Bev said, beginning to giggle.

"What, what?" Evelyn said.

Between giggles: "We could pretend we were at an adult cocktail party. Or a bar   ."

"I like it," Evelyn said. "I *like* it!"

"And we could try to pick somebody up!"

"What do you mean, pick somebody up?" Helen asked.

"Well, one of us could talk very sexy over the mike and invite the guy over," Bev explained.

"Could he find us?" I wanted to know.

"Oh, no, we'd cut out long before it ever got to that. We could just see if we can act well enough to carry it off for a while!"

"Oh, terrific!" Evelyn said. "Come on, let's go into Lenny's room. I'll be the picker-upper, because I can do a sexy voice." Robert rolled his eyes. "Now we need cocktail party noise. Get some glasses to clink together."

"I'll get 'em!" Skunky offered.

"And music. Play, Robert!"

Robert went back to the piano and played what he called "drunk music."

The rest of us sat down in front of the complicated-looking machine.

"Do you know how to work it?" Billy asked.

"I *think* so," Evelyn said.

"You *think* so!" Helen said. "After all that?"

"No, no, I do," Evelyn picked up the mike. "Now first you press this button on the mike to talk."

"How do we know who to talk to?" Diane wanted to know.

"Oooh, good question," Evelyn replied. "Let's flip the channel selector around and see if we can get an interesting-sounding person. Then we'll break in."

"How do you break in?" Barbara asked.

"I think you're supposed to say 'Breaker' and then a number."

"Yeah, 'Breaker One Nine'!" Billy cried.

"No, not 'one nine'," Evelyn said. "Nineteen is for mobile traffic who may need special directions or something. And it's always crowded. There's no chatting on Nineteen. We'll try some other channels. We just want to get someone's attention."

"Right," Bev said. "How many channels are there?"

"Well," Evelyn explained, "there are forty in the new sets. They cost a fortune. This one only has twenty-three."

Skunky came back with two jelly glasses and began clinking them together.

"Hey, it's not *Jingle Bells*, Skunky, for God's sake," Evelyn said. "Do it just every now and then."

"Okay."

"Turn the channel," Barbara said. "Let's listen."

Evelyn turned a dial and we were quiet.

"Breaker One Seven," we heard. "I need a Ten Thirteen going east on Northern State Parkway. Gimme road conditions and Smokey locations."

"What'd he say?" Billy asked.

"He wants to know about the traffic," Evelyn told him. "Smokey means the cops."

"We don't care about traffic," Helen said. "Switch the dial."

Evelyn did.

"Breaker One Five. This is Ding-Ding calling for Flyweight. Do you read me? Repeat: This is . . ."

"Ding-Ding and Flyweight?" I said, and clapped a hand over my mouth. "Can they hear me?"

"No, they can't hear you until I press the microphone button," Evelyn said.

Robert leaned in. "Maybe Ding-Ding and Flyweight are our guys," he said.

"What's your Twenty, Ding-Ding?" Flyweight was asking.

"I'm a base over at the Lynbrook Fire House. How about that meeting tomorrow night?"

"Can't. I'm heading over to the hospital now. The wife just had twins!"

"Some flyweight!" Robert said.

"Congratulations, Flyweight!" Ding-Ding said. "Ten-Four."

"Well, *they're* out," Diane said. "Try one more."

". . . nice modulatin' with ya," came the next voice. "I really didn't have anything to do tonight and I'm just lookin' for talk . . ."

"That's him!" Evelyn cried. "Robert, *play!* Skunky, *clink!*" They played and clinked.

"Breaker Two Three, Breaker Two Three," Evelyn said in the sexiest voice I ever heard. "This is Sweet Sue looking for the cute feller with nothin' to do tonight . . ."

There was a pause. Evelyn took her hand off the button and turned to us. "Come on, make crowd noises. You're all having a happy, drunken time."

I took one of Skunky's glasses and clinked it with him. We started to laugh. Helen began to sing and Barbara and Billy began to chatter to each other.

Evelyn pushed the button down and repeated her introduction.

"Hey, there, Sue," said the voice. "This is Heavy Dude. I'm your guy!"

Evelyn whispered, "Play louder, Robert!" and pressed down the button. "We're just havin' a little party here, Heavy," she oozed. "Can you hear the crowd?" She took her hand off the button and yelled, "Crowd, crowd!" We picked up our noise.

Button down. "You sound kinda lonely, Heavy," she said, and stifled her laughter. *We* could laugh because we were the crowd, and so we did. Robert swung into *Shine on Harvest Moon*.

"Well, yeah, Sue," Heavy Dude answered.

"How'dya like to come to our party?" Evelyn crooned.

"Oh, yeah, come to the party!" Barbara yelled into the mike.

"We *need* you," Bev wailed.

"Uh, what's your Twenty?" asked Heavy Dude.

"Our Twenty? It's uh . . ." Evelyn scratched the mike with her fingernail, then she hissed into it and lifted the button. "I didn't know what to tell him," she said, looking at the rest of us. "So I made static on the mike, like we were cut off."

"Can you get cut off on a C.B.?" I wanted to know.

"We just were," Evelyn said.

"Get him back," Barbara said. "Tell him your Twenty is 71 Coolidge Street."

"Who lives there?"

"Myrna Savitch."

"*Myrna Savitch!*" Everyone started to laugh.

"Who's Myrna Savitch?" I asked.

"Oh, she's this girl . . ." Helen started to tell me but broke up.

"She carries a Snoopy lunchbox," Diane choked.

"And she always has a hundred sharpened pencils in her briefcase," Bev added.

"And four packs of extra looseleaf paper," Billy said.

"And she's never missed a day of school in her whole entire life," Evelyn finished, and pressed down the button.

"Breaker: Sweet Sue for Heavy Dude, do you read me?"

"I read you, Sue. What happened?"

Just then, Robert began to play *Melancholy Baby*.

He started to sing it, too, but it came out more like a wail.

"Robert, shut *up!* You're overdoing it!" Evelyn yelled, but she forgot to take her finger off the button.

"Hey, what's this, a buncha kids?" Heavy Dude's voice got rougher all of a sudden.

"Uh, Ten-Four," Evelyn said, and clicked off. "Oh, Robert, you really blew it. You jerk!"

"It wasn't my fault," he said. "You kept your finger on the mike button!"

"I wish we could have sent him to Myrna's," Diane said.

Bev said innocently, "She might've liked him, who knows?"

∞

"I'll walk you home, okay?" Robert asked me, when it was time to leave.

"Sure."

Evelyn, on her way to the kitchen, stopped and looked at Robert. She didn't say anything.

"I'll be back," he said. "Don't worry, I won't leave ya with a big mess to clean up."

Evelyn nodded and continued on toward the kitchen.

"G'night, Evelyn. And thanks a lot. It was great," I called.

"Welcome," she called back. "Talk to you soon."

∞

It had rained while we had been inside and the street lights made everything glisten. The people across the street from Evelyn had carved their street number out of part of the hedge that grew in front of their house. It sat on top of the rest of the hedge like a hat: 430. It made me giggle.

"What's funny?" Robert asked. I pointed to the hedge.

"Oh, the Werners' hedge? Yeah, I remember when he carved that out with his shears and then cut the rest of the hedge lower. He really takes pride in that four-three-oh. It's actually a work of art." And then he started to giggle, too. "It's really ugly, isn't it?" Pretty soon we were laughing out loud. And then we stopped and it was quiet while we walked to the end of the block.

I said, "Hey, Robert?" at the same time he said, "What did you think of . . ." and we laughed again.

"You first," I told him.

"No, you. What were you going to say?"

"No, forget it," I said.

"Come on, Ronnie, I hate that. What were you going to say?"

"Well . . . I wanted to ask about your father. I was thinking of what you and Evelyn said about him yesterday."

"My father? Oh, he hangs around our house. He has a chair at the kitchen table, his own special coffee mug, and he bunks in with my mother."

"No, no kidding. Doesn't he like your friends or something?"

Robert laughed. "It's *me* he doesn't like."

"No, really," I said.

"Oh, I don't know if it's really *me*, exactly," he said. "I don't think he cares for anyone too much. He fights with my mother, he fights with my sisters, he's not too crazy about his job . . . There's only one thing he likes."

"What's that?"

"His hobby. He has this microscope he's always fooling around with and he's got this precious box of slides. Some he bought but most of them he made. Nobody's allowed *near* it, especially me."

"Why especially you?"

"Are you kidding? Ron, do you remember the way we first met?"

"Oh. Yeah. Spilled books."

"Ri-ight! I told my mother once that if the house was on fire and he could save one of us, he'd save the slides."

I looked at him to make sure he was kidding. "You're kidding," I told him.

He smiled. "It's no big deal, Ron. Some people are just very hard to get along with and he's one of them. You'll probably meet him sometime and you'll see for yourself. He'll definitely call you 'Ronald'. How'd you like the party?"

"Oh, it was fun. You sure can play piano!"

"Thanks. Do you have a piano?"

"Yeah, but I think it's still packed."

"Packed!"

"No, I'm joking. But we just moved in three weeks ago and we've only unpacked enough so my mother can paint, I can have clean underwear, and my father can get to work without being embarrassed. The rest of the stuff is still in boxes and you can hardly find anything. Anyway, my parents would flip over the way you play. As soon as we find the piano, you've got to come over!"

"Oh, sure," he said. "I love to impress parents. Then they say to their kids, 'Why don't you invite that nice boy over? What's-his-name, the one who plays the piano . . .' and I get to get out of the house."

We had arrived at my house, which looked kind of dark from the outside, but I figured it would be polite to ask Robert in.

"Oh, thanks, but I'd better get back to Ev's before she has a fit. I usually help her clean up and then we talk about everybody who was there." He smiled.

"What will you say about me?"

"If I was going to say anything bad about you, I wouldn't be telling you we talk at all! G'night, Ron!"

"'Night, Robert. Thanks."

∞

Crash. "Ow!"

"Ronnie?"

"No, it's a burglar," I said from the floor. "Is that why you moved all the packing crates in front of the door? You could've waited until I got home. Or turned on a light!"

"Oh, honey, I'm sorry." Daddy came running out of the bedroom in his pajamas and helped me up. "We thought you'd be using the back door. The light's on back there. You're not hurt, are you?"

"No," I answered, "but what do you say we spend tomorrow finishing this stuff? I wouldn't mind living out of boxes, if I just knew which boxes had what in them."

"You are right, young lady," Daddy said, his hand under my chin. "And if we plan to devote the *entire day* to working, we'll at *least* get a couple of good hours in!" I broke up. "How was the party?"

"Fun! We played with Evelyn's brother's C.B."

"Oh, he showed you how to work it?"

"No, he wasn't home. He wasn't supposed to know we used it."

Dad smiled. "Did you meet some nice kids? How about Skunky?"

"Yeah, he was there. There were some okay girls. And you should hear Robert Rose play the piano!"

"I hope we get to do that soon," Daddy said. "But how about getting some sleep? Your mom tried to wait up for you, too, but conked out a while ago."

"Yeah, okay. 'Night," I said.

But I wasn't tired. I was wide awake. I went into my room, didn't even bother getting undressed, and lay down on my bed.

It was a big room. The people who lived in the house before us had a son, and they'd put up wallpaper that had a bunch of sports figures on it. There was a row of baseball players, then a row of hockey players, then a row of football players. And it just kept repeating. Mom said it was too busy, but I liked it because I enjoyed counting how many players of each sport there were on each wall. Guess that sounds dumb. Anyway, I never finished counting a whole wall, I usually fell asleep.

I was more tired than I thought, because I didn't even get through a quarter of the wall. I fell asleep with the light on and my clothes on.

Chapter 4

Mom and Dad were still asleep at 9:00 the morning after the party, and I figured they'd probably stay zonked until about 11:00. Which meant we would all have a big brunch that would take us through about 12:30, then get dressed, and start working about 1:00. Break for lunch around 3:00, and then it was anybody's guess.

I decided to use the phone in my room and call Evelyn to thank her for the party. I wondered how late Robert stayed . . . Maybe she'd still be sleeping.

I called anyway. A boy answered the phone.

"Hi, is Evelyn there?" I asked.

"Yeah, whoozis?"

"Ronnie Rachman."

"Who?"

"Ronnie."

"Justaminute. *Evelyn!*" Right in my ear. Then I heard him mumble, "Jeez, some little boy on the phone for you. At 9:00 on Sunday morning. Jeez!"

Then I heard, "Shut up, Lenny. Hello?"

"Hi, Evelyn. It's Ronnie. Sorry if I disturbed your family."

"Oh, you didn't. Just Lenny. But everything disturbs him."

"Did he find out we used his C.B.?"

"No, or I'd've sure heard about it by now."

"Well, listen, I'm calling to thank you for the party. I really had a good time."

"Oh, good." Pause.

"Um . . . The kids I met are really nice. Diane seems like fun."

"Diane's okay," Evelyn said, "if you're into cheerleading."

There was something about her voice. "Are you mad at me or something?" I asked.

Quickly, "No, no. Why should you think that?"

"I don't know," I answered, "you just sound funny."

"Well, I'm not mad. Guess I'm just tired. Robert stayed until 12:30."

"*Twelve-thirty?* Weren't his parents mad? Or yours?"

"Mine were out until after one," she said. "Last night was Rotary Bingo. And Robert's sister, Caroline, called at about 11:00 to make sure he was still alive."

"Oh."

"What are you doing today?" she asked. "Wanna come over and bake bread?"

"Can't. Today we are definitely unpacking. We decided there are no more ways to get out of it."

"Have a wonderful time," she said. "I'll see you in Home Room on Monday."

"Yeah. 'Bye."

Maybe she is just tired, I thought. *Or I'm too sensitive.*

"Ronnie?" It was Mom, calling from her room. "Was that you on the phone?"

"I'm off now!"

"Little early on Sunday to be calling people, honey."

"Sorry I woke you, but now that you're up, maybe we can at least get the boxes off the piano!"

∞

The next week I saw Evelyn and Robert's act. They invited me to watch their rehearsal one day after school. I sat on the couch facing the piano, which Evelyn stood next to while she performed. Robert started playing background music, I think it was kind of a slow version of *Ease on Down the Road.* Then Evelyn eased on in from the kitchen and pantomimed looking into a window, reading a sign on a door, and then going in, closing the door behind her. After that she made like she was going through racks of clothes, looking at them, putting them back on the rack, and stuff like that. Robert swung into *By the Beautiful Sea* and Evelyn pantomimed tapping the shoulder of a salesgirl and asking for a bathing suit. That part was funny; she put her hands up to her body like she was asking for a teeny-weeny bikini and then the salesgirl handed her a gigantic tank suit! I could tell by the way she pantomimed taking it from the girl. Then she tried it on and ended up getting mad at the salesgirl and slamming out of the store. Robert was playing *Haven't Got Time for the Pain*.

I applauded like crazy when she exited into the kitchen.

"Ya hated it," she said, coming back out.

"No, I *loved* it!" I said. "Except . . ."

"Except what?" Ev wanted to know.

"Well . . . that part near the end . . . With the salesgirl. I couldn't tell why you were getting mad at her. And why you stormed out like that."

Robert frowned a little and shook his head. "See, Ev? I knew it wasn't smooth at that section." He bit his lip, thinking of how to fix it.

Evelyn looked at me. "It isn't clear there, huh? I was *trying* to show that the salesgirl wasn't giving me my right size, but actually, she *was*. What I was asking for was four sizes too small. The joke was that I was getting sore at *her* and she was *right*."

"Oh," I said.

"Maybe it needs a real salesgirl," Robert suggested. "You know, someone to play the salesgirl."

"A straight man!" Evelyn cried.

"A what?" I asked.

"A straight man. Someone to play off." She waved her hands. "How can I explain it? Like, a straight man is someone who is just doing straight stuff, while the comedian does the funny stuff. You know, in every comedy team, you have a guy who's funny, and the guy who takes it." She clapped her hands. "Like in 'I Love Lucy': Ricky isn't funny, but Lucy *is*. But Lucy couldn't be funny without Ricky in the story! See?"

I saw.

"Be my straight man!" she yelled.

I drew back. "Please, I love you, Evelyn, but I'm too young to get involved!" Robert laughed, but Evelyn was too wound up.

"Ronnie, do the act with us. Come on! You be the straight man."

"No way."

"Why? Oh, Ronnie, don't worry. It's pantomime! You won't have to open your mouth! Look, we'll make up a whole new one. Look, just try it. *Try* it! If you really aren't having fun, then I won't make you do it."

"Listen," I said, "this is my mother's bag. I mean, she's the arty one in the family. She's got painting friends and friends in the theater . . . *She'd* love it, but it's not for me."

"We can't use your mother," Evelyn said. "She's too old. Otherwise I'd call her."

Robert got up and came over to me. "I think

what Evelyn suggested is what the acts needs," he said. "Give it a try, Ron. The three of us will make it up together. Do it."

I didn't say yes right away, but they must have thought I did, because when I left they were patting me on the back and drinking a root beer toast to "The New Stars—the Three R's"—Racanelli, Rachman and Rose.

∞

"You really said you'd do it?" Mom asked when I told her.

"No. Yes. I think so."

"Well, I'm surprised!" she said. "But I think it's great. I do, Ronnie. Tell me about the act."

I told her what Evelyn had done and how they were going to re-write it with me, the straight man, playing off Evelyn.

"There are a lot of situations you can pantomime," Mom said, swiveling around on her stool. "Let's see . . ." she bit the nail on her pinky and leaned back. "You could do . . . How about pantomiming the Gym class, just the way it happened with Evelyn trying the climb the ropes?"

I tried to picture it. We could wear our Gym uniforms to add to the atmosphere. But wow, it would be hard to show rope climbing in pantomime. We could use great songs, though, like *Up, Up and Away* or *High Hopes*.

Mom was starting to get into it. "I know!" she

cried. "What about two girls at the movies? That would be easy to do. You know, squeezing through the row of seats, reacting to the scenes on the screen . . . What do you think?"

"I don't know. This really isn't my thing."

Mom took my face in both her hands and smiled at me.

"I know this is new for you, honey," she said, "but I think it'll be great fun. I really do. Why don't you call Evelyn and Robert and see what they think of the movie idea?"

They loved the movie idea. They wanted me to come right back to Evelyn's to re-work the new act, but I said we had time. We'd do it another day. I had funny feelings about performing . . . It made my stomach do weird things.

∞

A few days later, Beverly came running up to Evelyn and me in the halls just before lunch.

"Did you see the notice on the bulletin board?" she asked. "The first 'Y' get-together is Thursday night! Which one of our fathers will drive?"

"Bev really has a thing for Mr. Vincent," Evelyn said.

Bev just laughed. "If I were ten years older . . . no, *five*. That's all I need."

"That's not *all* you need, Beverly."

"Hey, are you going or what?"

"Sure. We'll go, won't we, Ronnie?"

I shrugged and nodded.

"If everybody goes, though, we'll probably need two cars. Lenny will drive one," Evelyn said, volunteering her brother.

"I guess my Dad will drive," I said. "I'm sure he won't mind. Thursday night?"

Thursday night.

∞

It turned out that only Evelyn, Beverly, Robert and I could go Thursday night, and my father drove us, so Lenny didn't have to.

Beverly was so excited she could hardly stand it. I mean, I thought Mr. Vincent was nice and all, but I didn't have dreams about him like Bev did. I wondered if it were true about him dating Miss Fisk and if Bev knew about it. Well, *I* wasn't going to tell her.

The "Y" wasn't too crowded when we got there. Just a few kids hanging around the refreshment table and I didn't know any of them. They looked older than eighth grade anyway.

"Look," Evelyn said and poked me.

I looked. "What?" I asked.

"Over *there*," she whispered, "near the juke box."

Miss Fisk was putting on records.

"See?" said Evelyn. "Karen Farber is *never* wrong."

I shook my head. "She could just be helping run the party," I suggested.

"Oh, sure," Evelyn said.

Bev was right about Mr. Vincent in jeans. He looked a lot younger and kind of cute. But he wasn't even looking at Miss Fisk.

"Hey, Rose!" Mr. Vincent called. "Am I glad to see you! I thought I'd have to listen to that juke box noise all night. Get over to that piano and do your thing!"

Robert looked at me and shrugged. "It's automatic," he said and smiled. "People look at me and think 'piano'. I usually walk over to it like a hamster climbs up on his wheel."

"That's kind of nice," I said.

"It is," he said, nodding, "unless you just discovered something you'd rather be doing." But he went over to the upright in a corner of the room and Miss Fisk turned off the juke box.

I looked around. There weren't any decorations, but this really wasn't supposed to be a party . . . just a kind of meeting to start off the year's program. It was just a large paneled room with photos on the wall of a bunch of kids doing summer-type things. I figured they were probably scenes from the "Y" camp.

The evening started dull and got duller. Evelyn and I spent most of our time talking about the movie pantomime. That is, *she* talked, and I tried to listen to her and to Robert's music at the same time.

What happened to un-dull the night was, when Evelyn got up to get more refreshments, this boy came over to me. He was a lot older than I was, maybe sixteen or seventeen.

"Hi, you new at Franklin?" he asked.

"Uh huh." I was a little nervous.

"What's your name?"

"Ronah," I said, avoiding the issue. "Uh, but they call me Ronnie for short."

"Hi."

"Hi." No name from him.

"Where d'ya live?" he wanted to know, and he wanted to know some more dumb things like that for a while until he finally came to the point.

"Hey, wanna go to a movie sometime?" was the point.

I really did get nervous then. I looked around for Evelyn but she was eating pretzels with Bev at the refreshment table. She was making eyes at me, but she didn't come over. Robert turned around on his piano stool every once in a while, but he didn't come over either.

Trapped. This was the first time I was ever really asked out. I mean for real, not just a movie with a bunch of kids who got together at the last minute. This was being *asked out*. And he was so old. How can you say no to an older guy?

All this stuff was running through my head in about thirty seconds while I decided what to say.

You don't say "I'll have to ask my mother" when you're talking to some sixteen-year-old. He probably drove, too. *Oh, jeez,* I thought, *what'll I say?*

"Hey, d'ja hear me?"

"Yeah, I heard you. What's your name?" I asked. A stall.

"Sheldon Mack."

Stall over. "Oh."

"Well?" he pushed. "Wanna go out?"

"Okay." Did I say okay?

"How about tomorrow night?" he said. My stomach dropped.

"You mean Friday?"

"Well, if today's Thursday, then it figures tomorrow's Friday. Yeah. Friday."

I could have said about a hundred things, I thought later, like it's too short notice and I already have plans, or I'm sorry, I expect to have a stomach ache, I always get them on Friday nights, or *anything*, but I said "okay, tomorrow night" and got up and went to the girls' room.

Followed immediately by Evelyn.

"What did *he* want?" she asked.

"Do you know him?"

"Of course," she said. "What did he say to you?"

"He asked me out."

"Sheldon *Mack?* Asked you out? How did you say no?"

"I didn't say no."

"Well, you didn't say yes . . ."

"I *did* say yes."

Evelyn put the palm of one hand up to her fore-head and the other hand over her heart. "Ronnie! Poor *baby!* Why didn't you check with Mama Evelyn! You can't go out with Sheldon Mack!"

"Why not?"

"For one thing, he hangs out at Blue Dell's," she said.

"So?"

"I *told* you about Blue Dell's. It's a bad crowd there. Most of them have been busted at least once. Sheldon was, I remember when it happened."

I swallowed.

"And he's a lot older than you, for another thing. And for the *third* thing . . ."

"What? What's the third thing?" I asked. I was beginning to shake.

"Guess what he expects from every girl he dates?"

"What does he expect?" I said quickly, not even thinking.

"Ronnie! What do you think he expects?"

"Oh. OH! Do you really think he expects that kind of thing from a thirteen-year-old?"

Evelyn didn't say anything.

"What am I going to do?" I wailed.

"When's your date?" she asked.

"Tomorrow night."

"Tomorrow! Boy he sure doesn't waste any time. Get the new girl right away! Come with me." She took my arm.

"No," I said, pulling back. "I'm not going out there until he's gone."

"Come *on*," she said. "I'll handle it."

I felt better. Evelyn would handle it.

We went over to the piano, where Robert was still playing, Evelyn's hand still yanking my arm.

"Guess what, Robert?" she said to him, "We're doubling tomorrow night. We're going out with Ronnie."

"Fine," he said, "but adding it up, it comes out a trio." He was playing *Feelings*.

"No, it's a double date. Ronnie's date is Sheldon Mack."

End of music.

"Sheldon *Mack?*"

"That was *my* reaction," Evelyn said. "She said yes before I got a chance to tell her."

"Sheldon *Mack?*" Robert repeated.

"Robert, you sound like a duck. Say something besides 'Sheldon *Mack*'," Evelyn said.

"My cousin Arlene went out with him," Robert said. "She said he had so many pairs of hands she couldn't find his face."

"What did she do?" I asked.

"She had to hit him. He wouldn't stop. She had to walk home."

"Oh, my God."

"Don't *worry*," Evelyn said. "Robert and I will go with you. We'll be with you every minute and *nothing* will happen."

Robert looked at Evelyn. "Has Sheldon bought this idea of yours, or haven't you told him yet?"

"We won't tell him. We'll just be at Ronnie's when he picks her up and that way he won't be able to say no. Especially in front of her parents."

"Oh, I can't," I cried, "I'd be too embarrassed."

"Look, suppose we do this," Robert said. "Suppose we be at the box office when you get there, coincidence, we happen to show up. And from then on, we just stick with you. We'll sit with you, get up to get candy with you, stretch with you, leave with you . . ."

". . . And fight him off with you," Evelyn finished.

"Okay," I said, worrying a lot, "but how about the ride home?"

"No problem," Robert said. "We'll just say that Evelyn and I don't have a ride home and he can drive us. Then you say you're sleeping over at Evelyn's and get out of the car with her."

"Brilliant," said Evelyn.

I was scared stiff.

Chapter 5

When I got home that night, Mom and Dad were in the den building shelves. That is, Daddy was building the shelves and Mom was standing around telling him how wonderful he was but wasn't the height of that bracket just a *little* off?

I told them I had a date, but I didn't tell them everything else. I felt just awful. I never hid anything from my folks before but I knew if I told them what Evelyn said about Sheldon Mack, they'd never let me go, and I couldn't face telling him that.

Mom was nervous about my going out with someone who drove a car, but Daddy said it would be okay, we were only going to a local movie and she shouldn't worry. I think he just said that because he thought he was helping me out; he didn't look too thrilled, himself.

Sheldon told me when he called on Friday afternoon that he wanted to see "King Kong." I said "terrific" and called Evelyn to tell her what box office to be in front of. It was playing at the Calderone.

I chewed a hole in the side of my cheek waiting for him to pick me up. He got there about 8:00, shook hands with my father, and mumbled something to Mom.

When we got in the car, I plastered myself up against the door, but he didn't even look at me, so I felt kind of stupid.

There was a line around the block, waiting for the movie. Immediately, I started chewing on the other cheek.

"Ahh, I don't feel like waiting on line," he said. "Let's go somewhere else." He started to put the car in gear.

"*No!*" I screamed.

He stopped and stared at me.

"Um, uh, I mean, I *really* want to see this movie," I said. "I've waited *weeks* . . . to see it . . . Honest!"

"Yeah," he said, "well, I have, too, but man, who needs a line like this . . . ?"

"It'll go fast!" I insisted. "These lines just zip by, you'll see. Come on."

It worked. He turned off the ignition and got out of the car. Now all I had to do was find Evelyn and Robert.

We got on the end of the line.

"What's the matter with you?" Sheldon said.

"Why?" I could feel my eyes get big. I thought, *can people smell fear like animals can?*

"You looking for someone? I mean, your head's movin' around like a spinning record."

"Don't be silly, who would I be looking for?" I asked.

"*Hi!* Isn't this *funny* running into you here, Ronnie! *Hi,* Sheldon!" In spite of being terrified, I almost started to laugh. Evelyn sounded like a cheery little chickadee. And there was Robert, glaring at Sheldon.

And there was Bev. And Skunky. And Diane and Billy Fenner. Oh, God.

"Hi, Evelyn," Sheldon mumbled.

All of them squeezed into line behind us, to the annoyance of some people who had just gotten there first.

"Boy, this is nice," Evelyn chirped. "Now we can all see 'King Kong' together! It's definitely the kind of movie you should see with a group, don't you think?"

Nobody said anything, so I piped up, "Oh, yes! That's what *everybody* says who's seen it. It's absolutely a group picture!"

Sheldon didn't have a single expression on his face. Nothing. I had no idea what he was thinking. But he said, "I don't think I wanna wait on this line after all, Ronnie."

Fear. Stomach jumping. Cheek bleeding all over my back teeth.

"Sure you do, Sheldon," I choked.

"Nah, come on, let's go." He took my arm and started to move out of line.

"Sheldon . . . I . . . I want to stay. Come on, Sheldon, look the line's moving quickly."

"Hey," Robert said. "She wants to stay, Sheldon."

"None of your business, Rosey," Sheldon growled.

"Oh, sure it is," Robert said. His voice cracked on "sure." "I mean, now that we're all together, uh, quadruple-dating like this."

"We're not with you," Sheldon said. "We're leaving."

"Why don't we vote," Bev put in. "Let's take a vote on whether to leave or stay."

"You're not comin' with us," Sheldon insisted.

"That's unfriendly, Sheldon," Evelyn said. "What's that old saying? 'Two's a drag and a group's a crowd'. Isn't that how it goes? Anyway, Bev's right. Let's vote. I'd like to stay."

"Me too," from Robert.

"How about going bowling?" Billy Fenner asked. "We could do that."

"I vote for bowling," Diane said.

"I'd like to go bowling," Skunky said. Evelyn glared at him.

"I *must* see this movie," Bev said.

"It's a tie," Billy said.

"I don't care what you guys want to do," Sheldon said. "Ronnie and I are . . ."

"A recount!" Evelyn cried. "Let's take a recount. Skunky looks like he wants to change his vote."

A man on the line in front of us turned around.

"I vote you go bowling," he said.

"Me too," said his wife.

Two kids in front of *them* joined in. "I think you should vote by secret ballot," said one girl.

"I think the whole line should vote," the other girl said.

The people in back of us who got nudged out when Evelyn and everybody arrived raised their hands. "We vote unanimously against your staying!" their spokesman said.

"Your vote can't count," Evelyn said politely. "You have an investment in the outcome. You get to move up in line."

"Sheldon," I said, getting a little courage, "this is a terrific movie. I want to see it, I really do. Please, Sheldon?"

"Okay," Sheldon said. "But I don't want to sit with these yo-yos."

I'll worry about that when we come to it, I thought.

∞

I didn't have to worry. They took care of it. Sheldon and I in the middle of the row. Robert next to me, Evelyn next to Robert. Skunky next to Sheldon, Beverly next to Skunky. Directly in back of us, Diane and Billy.

Every time Sheldon's arm started to move around

my shoulder, Diane would drop her popcorn on it. Or Billy would throw a coat over it. Or Robert would move *his* arm around my shoulder and touch Sheldon's and both would draw back. Or Beverly would kick Sheldon in the leg by accident as she stretched in her seat. He must have been furious but he didn't say anything. I leaned all the way over to my right, next to Robert, and worried about the ride home. Sheldon would never take them all home. Never. And the ride home was the worst part. I kept thinking, *I'm too small, I'm too young, I can't handle him.*

Everyone got up and left us as soon as the picture ended. Sheldon looked enormously relieved and I got terrified again. But when we got to his car, there they all were. Evelyn and Robert in the front seat, the other four in the back. They had fixed it so I didn't even have to sit next to the driver!

"Get outa my car!" was Sheldon's first reaction.

"We have no ride, Sheldon," Evelyn said. "My brother was supposed to be here but I just called home and my other brother said he forgot and took the car somewhere. You have to drop us off. Come on, Sheldon, don't be rotten."

Sheldon didn't say any more, just backed the car out of the lot and drove like crazy. To Robert's house first.

"Get out, Rose. Get going," he said.

"Oh, not here," Robert said. "I'm going to Racanellis'. We all are."

"Great," Sheldon said. "Get rid of you all at one stop." He drove right to Evelyn's in two minutes. And we all got out.

"Hey, what's this?" he asked, but he was a beaten man by this time.

"I'm staying here tonight," I said. I felt badly. Now that I was out of the car and it was really over, I felt sorry for Sheldon. It had been a mean trick after all. "I'm sorry, Sheldon, I thought I told you."

"Last time I mess around with a bunch of babies!" he growled, and drove away with a lot of muffler noise.

Evelyn hugged me and everyone laughed. I forgot about Sheldon. I was wondering if Robert put his arm around me in the movies as part of the game we were playing or if he was doing it because he wanted to.

That was the night I started thinking about Robert a lot.

Chapter 6

He was never on the school bus in the morning. I knew that his sister, Caroline, dropped him off on her way to work, so I relaxed on the bus. But my stomach started doing flips the minute the bus stopped at school. I looked at every face crossing the street from Harry's, or cutting across the yard.

Every time there was an accident in the halls, or I heard a crash behind me like books dropping, I turning around, thinking it might be him. Lots of times it was. I really began looking forward to the classes we had together, which were Social Studies, with Mr. Vincent, and Music, eighth period on Tuesdays and Fridays.

We got in trouble in Social Studies, which was nothing new for him, but it was for me. We were always talking. Or laughing. Teachers don't like that at all.

I always sat behind Robert and we would pass notes back and forth. One time I got this note that said, *Bet you a quarter Myrna Savitch won't lend you one of her freshly-sharpened pencils if you ask her.*

I started to giggle. Myrna sat across from Robert.

"Sssssst! Myrna," I whispered.

She wouldn't turn around.

"Myrna!" a little louder. Not a twitch from her. "I know you can hear me!" She wouldn't move. Robert started to crack up. I could see his shoulders shaking.

I hunched down behind him and tried again, whispering each word slowly and distinctly: "Myrna . . . I . . . have . . . you . . . covered . . . with . . . my . . . Star Trek . . . phaser gun. Turn . . . slowly . . . around . . . in . . . your . . seat . . . and . . . look . . . at . . . me. Or . . . I'll . . . *fire!*"

Robert fell over his desk.

Myrna whirled around in her seat and glared at me. "Ronnie Rachman, you leave me alone. And don't talk to me in class!"

"Myrna, I'm surprised at you." It was Mr. Vincent. "Please stop your talking while someone is trying to recite."

Myrna's face was Shock City. She turned around and gave me such a scowl . . .

I smiled and waved at her. She threw a pencil at me and got yelled at again, which made her cry.

"Robert Rose," Mr. Vincent said, "are you annoying Myrna?"

"Who me?"

Myrna pointed. "It was Ronnie!"

"Ronnie?"

"I'm sorry," I said innocently. "I wasn't annoying her. She got annoyed all by herself."

That was okay to say, because that could very easily happen with Myrna Savitch. Anything could annoy Myrna.

"That's enough now, okay?" Mr. Vincent said. "I don't want to have to start changing seats around. Got it? Now let's continue. Cindy?"

I passed a note to Robert. It said: *I've got the pencil. I win. Pay up.*

A note came back that said: *You lose. I said you had to ask her, not get it thrown at you.*

Note from me: *Rat fink!*

Note from him: *Cheater!*

Note from me: *Your father uses a whoopee cushion!*

Note from him: *How did you know?*

"Robert, move your things to the last desk in the row," from Mr. Vincent.

∞

Everybody liked Mr. Vincent. He was a good teacher and he was great at the "Y," but he had a few expressions that he used all the time that Robert and I started to listen for. His favorite was "Spoon-fed Social Studies." He would say, for example, "I don't want you guys to turn into non-thinking Xerox machines. I don't want you to put *my* facts on a piece of paper, use your brains! You want everything spoon-fed. I'm not giving you spoon-fed Social Studies!"

A kid would say, "Mr. Vincent, would you say that the Equal Rights Amendment should be a federal law? My father says . . ."

And Vincent would say, "Uh uh uh! 'Spoon-fed Social Studies'! I don't care what your father says or what your great-aunt Matilda says and you shouldn't care what I say. We'll dig up the facts on all sides and you make up your own mind!"

Note from Robert: *After school today—my house, your house or Evelyn's house?*

Note from me: *Why do you want spoon-fed leisure time? Make your own decision!*

Note from me: *Should Evelyn and I dress alike in the act?*

Note from Robert: *What do you want, spoon-fed costume designs? See what looks best and make up your own mind!*

And like that. We said "spoon-fed" so much, even my parents picked up on it. "Spoon-fed" became Robert's and my first inside joke.

Chapter 7

Around the second week in October, we still didn't have a finish for the act. We'd worked on most of it, and we had some pretty funny parts, but we didn't know how to end it like Evelyn wanted to, "leaving the audience laughing." We decided to work after school at Robert's, because Evelyn's brother, Stewart, the oldest one, was using their house to practice with his rock group, and our piano hadn't been tuned since we moved. Robert suggested his house because his father was away all week on business. He was a salesman. He sold laboratory equipment or something.

When we got there, Mr. Rose's car was out front, which seemed to throw both Evelyn and Robert.

"Doesn't he always take his car?" Evelyn asked.

"Yeah."

"Well, maybe it broke down and he rented one," she suggested.

"Maybe," from Robert.

"Well, let's go in and see," I said.

Robert said, "Why don't I . . ." and stopped. "No, okay, let's go in."

Mr. Rose was in the living room with his back to us. He didn't turn around when the door opened, but I could see the back of a robe, and pajamas sticking out of the collar.

Robert mouthed, "He must be sick."

Evelyn mouthed, "See you later." She waved four fingers at us and slipped out the front door.

I was really wondering how bad it could be, when Robert indicated with his head and his thumb that if I wanted to take off too, it would be okay with him.

I shook my head and we walked into the room very slowly. I had a weird feeling that I ought to be on guard or something. I wasn't really scared, but Robert was white. No, green. Both.

His father was watching TV with his feet, in torn leather slippers, propped up on a footstool. He didn't look at us even when we were standing in front of him.

Robert coughed and said, "Hi, Dad. How come you're home?"

Mr. Rose looked up and saw me.

"Goddamn it, Robert, do you have to bring in the whole neighborhood when I'm trying to get a little rest? Can't you see I'm sick? Get out of here!"

"Yeah," Robert said, taking my arm and backing out of the room. "Right."

His fingers on my arm were ice cold. He was still backing out until we got to the stairs near the front door and then he quickly turned and raced up, pulling me right behind him.

We went straight to his room, where he quietly closed the door, waiting until he heard the click in the latch before he seemed to relax even a little.

He looked at the floor for a long time until finally he looked at me and cleared his throat.

"Hey, I'm . . . sorry about that," he said and coughed again.

"That's okay," I said and meant it. I felt terrible for Robert but my own feelings weren't hurt or anything. "Honest. Don't worry about it."

"Well . . ." he said. "Um, sit down."

I looked for a place, but the only spot that was really sit-able was the bed, so I sat on that. I began to examine the room. Robert's room. I wanted to be able to picture him in it when I was alone.

The room sure was a mess. On the floor was a record player, with records piled up all around it. Next to that was a pile of clothes with some books on them and more clothes on top of the books.

There was a desk, which I was sure he didn't use because there was so much junk on it and under the desk was a bunch of rolled-up socks. I liked it. It was lived-in.

I said, "Hey, Robert," at the same time he said, "Hey, Ronnie," and we both smiled.

"That picture," I said, "over the desk. That's really nice."

"Oh, 'Little Sad Sack'?" he asked. "Yeah, I've had that picture since I was a baby, I guess, but I never took it down. I sort of like it, too. Reminds me that everybody's got problems!"

In the painting was a little boy, about three years old. He had big, dark eyes, and a huge tear was running down the side of his face. On the ground next to his feet was a toy truck, with the whole front caved in.

"Poor little guy," Robert said and grinned. "I keep telling him not to cry . . . Things can only get worse!"

"Listen," I said, "Please don't worry about my feelings. It's not me he hurt. Your father's hard to get along with. You already said that, so okay, we'll stay clear of him as much as we can if that's the way it has to be."

He looked relieved. "Evelyn and I kid about him a lot. It makes it easier to take. Well, look, forget it. There's something I wanted to ask you . . ."

"What?"

"Have you seen Sheldon Mack since That Night?"

"Yeah, last week at the 'Y'. You were there, remember?"

"I know," he said, "but I was playing piano. I didn't really see if you were talking to him or not."

"Are you kidding? I avoided him as much as he avoided me!"

"Good," Robert said and smiled. I felt terrific. "I'm not gonna play as much down there. I want to be more in touch with what's happening."

That made me feel so nice that I just smiled and took a deep breath, because I didn't know what to say. I tried to think of something but all that came to mind was Sheldon Mack, since that's what we had just talked about.

"Robert, isn't Sheldon too old for the 'Y' program?"

"Sheldon's not the only older kid down there. Didn't you see some of his friends? They come because it's another place to hang out if other places are closed and also . . ."

"Also what?"

"Also they can pick up younger girls . . ."

"Yeah."

"And . . . you know."

"No, what?"

"You know about Blue Dell's."

"So?"

"So some of them are dealers. They might find some young kids at the 'Y' that they can turn on."

"Sell them dope?"

"Uh huh. I don't think they're into very hard stuff. Grass and hash, mostly. At least as far as I know. But some of them have been busted. Sheldon didn't try any of that with you, did he?"

"Uh uh."

"Well, I don't know of anyone in our class they've gotten to. Or who got to them. But it's a big class. In *our* group there's no one, I guess."

"You guess?"

"I couldn't swear to it, Ronnie, but I don't think so. I mean, *Skunky?*"

We laughed. Robert got up and looked through his records. "Would you like to hear a show? Or popular? Or how about some jazz?"

"You pick something. Make up your own mind! What d'ya want, spoon-fed music?"

He grinned at me, "You're gonna pay for the smart remark, Rachman," he said. "Just for that you get an afternoon of Sousa marches!"

"I don't believe you've got an afternoon of Sousa marches in that collection," I said. "I bet you don't even have one record of a Sousa march."

"Smug, aren't you," he said, throwing a rolled-up ball of socks at me which I ducked. "Well, it just so happens, you're right. Not one Sousa march. But you know what's just as bad? Thirty minutes of jazz violin! And that I've got!"

I clutched my stomach and rolled over on the bed. "I give up. How 'bout some jazz?"

Robert rummaged. "Hey, here's some old Bessie Smith blues. What about that?"

"No," I said. "I'm not in a blue mood any more."

∞

That same week there was a meeting at the "Y" after supper to discuss plans for a Halloween party. Evelyn and Robert and I were on the entertainment committee. We thought that since the Methodist Church show and the Halloween party came on the same weekend, we would do our act both nights, for each event, if Mr. Vincent agreed.

We all met at Evelyn's. Lenny was driving. He was glad to get out of his house because it was Mr. Racanelli's poker night at home, and they never let Lenny play. Evelyn said they used to let him play but he always won, so Mr. Racanelli set an age limit of thirty for all players.

Beverly was the head of the decorating committee, so she was there, and Helen and Skunky were doing refreshments, so they were along, too. That meant seven of us in Lenny's Datsun. I was the smallest, so I sat in the back on Robert's lap.

"I'm not playing piano tonight," Robert said. "I never get to talk to anybody when I'm playing."

"What?" asked Evelyn from the front seat.

"I said I'm not playing tonight."

"Well, you won't have to," she said. "It's a meeting, not a party."

I tried to put my weight on my feet so I wouldn't be too heavy on Robert.

"Are you uncomfortable?" he asked, shifting around.

"No, are you? Am I too heavy?"

"Oh, no," he said. "No, not at all."

"What are you guys mumbling about back there?" Evelyn said.

"Nothing, we're just getting comfortable," I told her. I hoped Lenny would drive slowly so I could spend more time on Robert's lap.

∞

"Well, if it isn't the Dynamic Duo," Mr. Vincent called from across the room as we all walked in.

"What duo?" Evelyn asked. "There are six of us."

"He means Robert and me," I told her. "Seventh period Social Studies. We've been getting in trouble."

"Oh, well, that's par," Evelyn said. "Robert's trouble cloud is over your head now, too."

I didn't tell her that it was just as much my fault. "I guess so," I said.

"Speaking of Dynamic Duos," Evelyn said, "there's Fisk!"

She was in a huddle with Mr. Vincent near the piano. Boy, did she look terrific. She had on a gauzy kind of shirt over really tight straight-leg jeans, and she was wearing these huge gold hoop earrings.

"Evelyn?" I asked.

"What?"

"Wanna get our ears pierced?"

"What brought *that* on?"

"Look at Fisk. Don't those gold hoops look neat?"

"Not on me," she said. "I'd look like a two-wheeled truck. Come on, let's get this show on the road." Evelyn began to move chairs together so we could sit in a kind of circle to discuss our plans. Miss Fisk and Mr. Vincent sat together on the refreshment table, facing us.

We told them the idea of the act we wanted to do, but not enough to give anything away. Skunky talked Evelyn into making cheese puffs and Bev said she'd make a horror house if she could get about ten kids to help her. Robert took off his shoes and rested both his feet on my back, which Evelyn said was gross.

When the meeting was over, Evelyn went to call Lenny to pick us up and I helped Miss Fisk fold the chairs and throw away paper cups and napkins.

"You seem to be getting along just fine in your new school, Ronnie," she told me.

"Oh, I am," I said. "I like it a lot."

She nodded. "You've made a lot of friends in a short time. That must be a very nice feeling."

"It is . . . I really like your earrings."

"Thank you," she said and laughed. "They were a present."

I made a silent bet they were from Mr. Vincent.

"I'd like to wear earrings like that, but I think I'm too short. You have to be tall to carry it off," I said.

"Well, large earrings do seem to look better on larger people. But there are plenty of other styles that look wonderful on smaller girls."

"Really? Like what?"

"Tiny hoops are pretty," she said, "or buttons . . . Practically anything that isn't enormous and makes you look weighed down." She took one of my ears in her hand. "Honey, your ears aren't even pierced."

"I know, but they will be soon," I said.

She laughed again. "Well, just make sure you don't do it yourself."

"Miss Fisk?"

"Hm?"

"Is it really exercise that gives you such a good figure?"

"Ronnie, I want to take you home with me," she said. "You're the biggest ego-builder I've met in ages. Yes, exercise sure helps. And eating the right foods. You know all that garbage they teach you in school?"

"Yeah?"

"Well, it's all true, honey. Believe it. Sleep, diet and exercise. And you'll grow up to look just like me!" She let out a whoop and swiveled her hips.

"Tan and all?" I asked, and she roared.

Chapter 8

I finally nagged Mom into getting the piano tuned and Robert and Evelyn came over one day after school to practice the act. We also really needed Mom's help to put an ending on it.

Mom was painting, naturally, when we got there. We went into the studio and watched her. Nobody said anything because we didn't know what to say.

Finally Evelyn spoke up. "What do you call it, Mrs. Rachman?"

" 'Oktoberfest'," Mom said.

"Oh."

"Why 'Oktoberfest'?" Robert asked.

"Good question," Mom replied. "Why do you think?"

"Well," Robert said, backing up a little and staring at the picture, ". . . the colors are all fall colors. I mean, red, yellow, brown . . ."

"That's what I was thinking," Mom said. "The title just came to me when you asked."

"Listen, Mom," I said, "we're going into the living room to rehearse, and when you can break away, why don't you come in and see if you can help us?"

"Oh, sure," she said. "Love to. Help yourself to a snack first."

"Great," Evelyn said, and headed for the kitchen, where she put down a half of a box of Burry's Best and two glasses of milk. Robert and I just had milk, which he knocked over trying to pull the box of cookies out of Evelyn's hand.

After we worked about forty-five minutes, Mom came in, smelling of turpentine.

"Mom, we do all this stuff that two girls might do in a movie, but when it comes to the end, it just dies," I complained.

"Yeah," Evelyn went on. "The movie's over, and then we just get up and walk out. How can you make that funny?"

"Robert's played ten different kinds of 'walking' music, but nothing seems right," I said.

Mom flopped down on the couch and scratched her head. "Let's see . . ." she said, staring into space . . . "End of movie, end of movie . . . Hey, what if you don't get to the end of the movie?"

"What do you mean?"—a chorus of three.

"Suppose with all the carrying-on you're doing, you get thrown out by the usher? Then you can walk out in a huff!"

"Yeah!" Robert cried. "You can give the usher a big argument in pantomime and stalk out! I could play, uh, hmmm . . . *50 Ways to Leave Your Lover* or *Rolling Home* or . . .''

". . . *The Party's Over*," Mom offered.

"Fantastic!" Evelyn cried. "What we'll do is, in the middle of one of our arguments, where you're trying to keep me quiet, Ronnie, I'll pantomime feeling a tap on my shoulder and I'll look up, see the usher, and then tap you. You turn around in your seat, see the usher too, and then we both join forces instead of fighting with each other, and start fighting with him!"

"Then," Mom said, "how about this: you both pantomime that he's grabbed you by the elbows and is hustling you out of the theater. So you exit in kind of an awkward position, because he's holding onto you."

"That's sensational, Mrs. Rachman. Thanks a lot!" Evelyn beamed.

"Any time," Mom said, getting up. "I'm awfully glad I could help. I'm not going to see it in rehearsal, I'll wait for the big night." And she returned to the studio.

"Robert, we need a theme song," Evelyn said. "That's the only thing that's missing."

"When would that come?" Robert asked.

"You play it right after we're introduced and then again when we come out for our bow."

"Bow?" I said.

"Well, of course, dummy. Doesn't every actor take a bow after his thing?"

"Do we have to?" I asked, caught Evelyn's look and nodded. "We have to," I said.

"And we'll need a theme song because that'll be the song we'll get known by," she went on. "Every time we do another act, we'll use the same song at the beginning and at the end."

"Another act?" I said. "What other act?"

"Oh, after this we'll be in demand," Evelyn explained. "Word will get around. From the Methodist Church to the Elks Club Annual Dinner Dance, to the Rotary Club's Roast Night, to the . . ."

"Today the Methodist Church, tomorrow the world," Robert said. "Ev, you sure think big!"

"It's the only way to think, Robert," Evelyn said. "Anyway, aren't you guys having fun doing this? Come on, the truth."

Robert smiled and nodded. I nodded too, but I think my fun was being with both of them, especially Robert. It *was* a funny pantomime and we had had lots of laughs putting it together. I didn't want to think about doing it in front of an audience—the thought of that gave me a stomach ache, and the weekend of the 30th was getting closer and closer.

"How about *Love Will Keep Us Together?*" Robert said.

I looked at him. "Huh?"

"For the *theme!* Remember that song? *Love Will Keep Us Together?* That's a good song for the three of us, don't you think?"

"Yes," Evelyn said. "That's a good song."

∞

The next day after school, I went to Evelyn's. Robert had a piano lesson, but he was coming by afterwards so we could rehearse.

"I forgot to ask you," Ev said, making herself a bologna and cheese sandwich. "Did anything happen with Robert's father yesterday?"

"Like what?"

"I mean, was he his usual adorable self, or did he leave you alone?"

"What's with him, Evelyn? Has he always been so nasty?" I asked.

"Harlan William Rose was born nasty," she said. "When he came out he didn't cry like other babies, he twitched his moustache and bawled out the doctor for having cold hands. He used to scare me when I was little, but now when Harlan's home I just stay away from the Rose garden."

Mrs. Racanelli came into the kitchen. She usually did volunteer work at the hospital in the afternoons, but that day she was home.

"What's this about Harlan Rose?" she asked, opening the refrigerator.

"Nothing. Ronnie met him yesterday."

Mrs. Racanelli poured herself a Tab. "How is Harlan these days?" she said to me.

"He's sick. He has the flu. Or a cold, or something," I told her.

"Hmph," she muttered on her way upstairs. "So something finally bit *him!*" and she was gone.

"He's got this terrific reputation," Evelyn said. "Honestly, my mother wouldn't say a bad word about anyone, I mean it. But she's still mad about the time she suggested that Robert take piano lessons because he seemed so talented, and ol' Harlan screamed at her for twenty minutes on the phone."

"What for?"

"Oh, for turning his son's little head toward 'sissy stuff' like music, and for telling him how to spend his own hard-earned money. He said if she wanted Robert to have piano lessons then she should pay for it."

"You're kidding!"

"I'm not. You know who pays for his lessons? His sister, Caroline. She's a nurse at the hospital where my mother works and she told her."

"I'm surprised they even have a piano, then," I said.

"Believe me," Evelyn said, shaking her head, "he'd love to get rid of it. But it belonged to Robert's mother before they got married and there's no way she'd part with it."

We were quiet for a while. I kept thinking how lucky I was. Both my folks always encouraged everything I tried to do, even if I was lousy at it. Like doing this act, for example.

"Evelyn, how am I in the act?"

"Fine. Great. What do you mean?"

"I mean, am I doing it right? Am I being a good straight man?"

Evelyn said, "The only way we'll know that is if the audience laughs in the right places. But *I* think you're just great. Really."

"*Ev? Ron?*" It was Robert. "*Kitchen?*"

"*Yep!*" from Evelyn. "But we're coming out! Get over to the piano bench!"

"Work, work, work!" he complained, as we came in.

After we had done the act twice, Robert let his hands fall limply on the piano, sounding a terrible chord.

"Oh, God, it's happened; he's lost his touch," Evelyn cried dramatically. "The clock strikes 4:00 and he loses his talent!"

"That's right," Robert said weakly. "Unless I'm fed instantly the magic fingers will not work."

Evelyn got up quickly. "Oh, you hungry? I'll be right back." She went into the kitchen and I sat down next to Robert on the piano bench. He kept on playing *Love Will Keep Us Together*.

After a minute he said, "I lied."

"About what?"

"I'm not hungry. I just wanted to be alone with you for a minute. There's something I want to ask you," he said.

"What?"

But he went on playing. "This is like in the movies," he said. "Now we're at the part where the girl sings softly into the piano player's ear."

"If I sang softly into your ear," I said, "your hands would freeze on the keys."

"Can't you sing?" he asked.

"Oh, I love to sing. But I sound like a cross between Tammy Wynette and a hungry cat."

"Come on, sing," he said. "Sing *Love Will Keep Us Together*."

I sang the first verse with him while he played.

"Hey, that's not bad," he said. "Look, we've got a new act!" Both of us looked toward the kitchen and stopped.

"Ronnie, what I wanted to ask you was—wanna go to the movies Saturday night?"

"The three of us?"

"The two of us."

This time only I looked at the kitchen door. "Yeah," I said quietly, "I would."

"Hey, will you kindly give me a hand?" came a yell from the kitchen. "How am I supposed to balance three bologna sandwiches and three Cokes?"

We were chomping into the sandwiches when Evelyn said, as I had a feeling she would, "Well, what do you want to do this weekend?"

Eating gave us a chance to not answer her right away. I felt funny. I know Robert felt funny. Neither of us wanted to hurt Evelyn's feelings. She was my first and closest friend in Uniondale and if she were mad at me I couldn't stand it. And what about Robert? She'd known him all her life. What if she thought I was breaking up their friendship? I wouldn't do that even if I could and I definitely couldn't anyway.

I hated that bologna sandwich.

"Oh, wow, it's nearly 4:30!" I said, getting up. "Gee, I've got to get home!"

"Oh, okay," Evelyn said. "I'll call you tonight."

I left them both sitting there and got out. Where I was, was in a terrible position. Somebody was going to have hurt feelings, there was no way around it, and it seemed to be up to me to pick which one of the three of us was going to have them.

Well, I had to talk to Robert first. That much seemed clear.

Daddy was home when I got there. Surprise.

"What are you doing home?" I asked. "Where's Mom?"

"Shopping," he answered, stretching. "Yeah, I took an early train. Felt bushed. I'm going to take a nap. How're you? Uh oh, not good."

"How can you tell?" I said, smiling in spite of feeling crummy.

"Oh, because you have this special wrinkle that starts on your forehead and crawls down both cheeks whenever you're feeling bad. It's a dead giveaway."

I gave him a weird look.

"And besides, you didn't jump up and down and yell 'Daddy, you're home early!' and give me a hello kiss *immediately!*"

I jumped up and down, yelled "Daddy, you're home early!" and gave him a hello kiss as immediately as I could.

"Okay," he said, "now what's wrong?"

I told him the whole thing. "So what should I do?" I asked.

He made me laugh by saying, "Ah, spoon-fed answers, right?"

"Right!"

"Well, what is it you *want* to do?" he said.

"I wanna go out with Robert. Alone."

"All right then . . ."

"But I don't want to hurt Evelyn's feelings."

"Uh huh. Well, is it possible to go out with Robert without hurting Evelyn's feelings?"

"I don't think so."

"Well, honey," he said, "I'm going to take a nap."

"Hey, wait a minute, you haven't told me what to do."

"I can't do that, Ronnie," he said. "You have to decide which is more important to you first. Then you have to talk to the person involved and explain what you're doing and why in a way that will hurt his or her feelings least. And the phone's ringing. Good night."

It was Robert. He hadn't said anything to Evelyn, either, and wanted to know which one of us should tell her that we were going out alone Saturday night.

"Robert," I said, "we'll have to go out, the three of us."

"Ronnie, come *on!*" he said. He sounded angry. "Don't pull a 'Sheldon Mack' on me. I asked you out, boy to girl. We're not bringing along a third party!"

"Robert, this 'third party' happens to be our best friend."

"I know."

"Well, you've known her longer. How do you think she'll feel about it?"

"She'll be mad at first," he said, ". . . and then she'll get over it."

"She may get over it with you, but I'm not such a lifelong friend. Maybe she won't get over it with me."

There was a pause on the other end. "Yes, she will," he said finally, "because she needs you in the act."

"That's a crummy reason," I said.

"But it's a reason," he answered. "She'll make herself get over being angry or hurt because of the act and because she really likes us both."

I didn't say anything.

"Look, Ron," he continued, "we'd better get this

out in the open now. I really want to go out with you and I don't want Ev to be there every time. This is going to come up again and again if we put it off."

"Have you ever gone out with someone without her along?" I asked.

"No."

"She's calling me tonight and I'll tell her then," I said.

"Call me right back when you're through," he answered.

∞

I couldn't eat supper that night, waiting for Evelyn to call. I bit my nails and the inside of my cheeks and every time the phone rang I jumped. Drove my poor parents crazy. Finally, about 8:30, she called.

"Hi, what's happening? . . . Are you there?"

"Uh huh."

"Listen," she said, "I just spoke to Helen and guess what?"

"Evelyn, I have to tell you something . . ."

"What? Don't tell me, you got cold feet about the act!"

"No, it's . . . Um, about Saturday night . . . Robert asked me to go out with him and I thought I'd like to."

Pause. "You mean just the two of you?"

"Well, yeah. Please don't be mad. It's not that

we don't want to be with you or anything like that, it's just . . . like . . . a date."

"A real date? With *Robert?*"

"Uh huh. Evelyn, please don't have hurt feelings, it's nothing to do with our friendship at all. I mean it."

"Okay, well, do what you want," she said. "I have to hang up now, I have about a ton of homework."

"Evelyn, wait a minute . . ."

"I really have to. 'Bye." Click.

I was so upset I didn't even call Robert. He called about 10:00, which aggravated my mother no end.

"How'd she take it?" he said immediately.

"Not great. Listen, I can't talk now. It's late and I feel awful."

"I'll talk to her tomorrow. But it's all right about Saturday, right?"

"Right."

Chapter 9

Evelyn didn't talk to me in Home Room. She looked miserable. I *felt* miserable. Before French class started, I pulled her aside.

"I have to talk to you," I said.

She said, "Talk."

"I really can't stand," I began, "to have anything happen to our friendship. It's too good a thing to be broken up. I like Robert a different way from the way you do—I mean, you two grew up together so you wouldn't think of him as anything but a friend. Only it's different for me. And it doesn't mean either of us like you any less than we did yesterday."

She looked at me for a long time. Then she said, "You mean you really *like* old bumbling *Robert?*"

I didn't know how to take *that*. Finally, I just said, "Yeah."

"I can't imagine thinking of him that way," she said.

"I know *you* can't," I said, "but that doesn't mean someone else can't. And we're still all friends. Best friends. I wouldn't hurt you for anything."

She finally nodded. "It's not going to be the same," she said, "but if that's the way it is, that's the way it is. And if you stop liking each other 'that way', will you still do the act with me?"

"Of course."

She was right. Somehow, it wouldn't be the same.

∞

Robert picked me up at my house Saturday night. Very formal. Usually, we would meet at wherever we were going. We decided to go to the Casa Loma and split a pizza. My father offered to drive us, but we wanted to walk. It was a cool fall night, but not cold, and we felt like walking, even though the Casa Loma was about a mile and a half away.

For the first quarter mile, we didn't even say anything to each other. I was thinking about Evelyn.

"How's she treating you?" I said to him.

"Who, Ev? She's all right. I told you she'd get over it," he said. "Are we going to talk about Ev all night?"

"No, I was just wondering." All of a sudden we didn't have anything to talk about. *Maybe*, I thought, *we should write notes to each other*.

Then Robert stopped walking. I stopped, too, and I looked at him. He put his hand into his pocket and pulled out a pack of cigarettes with matches stuck in them. He put a cigarette in his mouth and lit it. Very casually. If he was trying to look cool, he blew it because when he touched the match to the end of the cigarette he closed his eyes and winced.

I put my hands on my hips. "What do you think you're doing?" I asked.

"Oh, just . . . having a . . . cig . . ." That was as far as he got. He started to cough so hard I had to take the cigarette out of his hand for him and smack him on the back. I started to laugh and then he started to laugh, but he was still coughing so the sounds were really weird. The tears were streaming down his face.

I stomped on the cigarette. "Can you talk?" I asked.

Nod, choke.

"Well, what was that all about?"

"It didn't work," he said. "I was going to do my Mr. Sophisticated number. I practiced at home with three cigarettes and I didn't cough once! Well . . . once."

I couldn't help laughing, but I said, "Robert, that was really dumb. *Dumb*, Robert!"

"I know. But I had this terrific image of myself, casually lighting a cigarette, blowing smoke into the night air, impressing you with my coolness. If I could grow a quick beard, I'd do it."

I looked at my watch. "You have five minutes."

"Okay," he said and pulled on his chin.

"Cigarettes are bad for your health," I said.

"Well, what's more important, health or appearance?" he said. "Is a goatee beginning?"

I looked. "No, but your chin is getting longer."

"Guess I can't do it in five minutes. Give me to the end of the evening. Can you dance?"

"No," I said. "Can you?"

"No."

"Good," we both said.

The Casa Loma wasn't crowded. It was too early for the Saturday night pizza mob, who usually came in *after* dates. We ordered a large pizza with everything on it except anchovies. It was fantastic.

"*Ow!*" Robert yelled.

"What's the matter?"

"I burned off the entire roof of my mouth with this pizza," he said, panting. "Quick, gimme your water, I drank mine."

He reached across the table for my glass and knocked it over into my lap. I jumped up as the ice water soaked through my jeans and down my leg.

"Oh, gee, oh God, Ron, I'm sorry, hey, let me help . . ."

"No, no!" I cried, "for God's sake, don't help! Wait a minute . . ."

The waiter appeared with a terry cloth towel and I mopped myself up while Robert sat whimpering apologies at me. It cracked me up. Then it cracked him up.

"I knew I would do that," he said. "I just knew it was a question of time. Would it be spilling something or dropping something? My sister, Caroline, voted for spilling and my baby sister, Laura, voted for tripping. Damn, damn, damn!"

"Well, they could both win," I said. "The evening is still young."

"Don't say that," he said. "I'm finished for the night. What do you want to do after the pizza? Don't say go over to Ev's."

"I wasn't going to say that."

"I know, let's go have ice cream sundaes!" he said.

"After pizza? *Blagh!*"

"Why not? And after that we'll go over to Sun Wing for Chinese food. Egg rolls!"

"You're really crazy," I told him. "You're doing an Alka Seltzer commercial."

"How about bowling?"

"Are you kidding, Robert Rose? I wouldn't trust you anywhere near my feet with a bowling ball!"

"Well, whaddya want, a spoon-fed date? You think of something," he said.

"Let's hitchhike to Vermont," I said, shrugging.

"Great. Marvelous," he said. "Let's go."

"What?"

He took a bite of pizza as he reached for his jacket behind him. "Come on, let's go. How far is it, seven hours?"

I panicked. "Sit down, Robert," I said, pulling

on the sleeve. I pulled too hard. His arm came down and his hand went smack into the pizza. I laughed so hard I cried. He stood there with tomato sauce, cheese, meatballs and pepperoni all over his hand and sleeve. It did me in.

"That one was mine!" I screeched. "All mine, not yours at all. It's rubbing off on me!" I had to gasp for air.

"And you even supplied the wet towel," he said, picking it up. "How kind."

"Now we're even. At least so far," I said. "Come on, let's go."

Outside on the street, he said, "I can't hitch to Vermont wearing meatballs and pepperoni. What would people say?"

"They'd say, 'Look at the crazy New Yorker. Maybe it's a fad and we should all wear it!' "

"I still think it was a great idea," Robert muttered. "Let's put that on a list of things to do."

"Okay, it's on the list. But that still leaves tonight. What time is it?"

"9:30. Do you have a curfew?"

"Well . . ." I said, "Mom didn't say anything, but I think if I was home by 11:00 it would be all right . . ." My real thought was probably closer to 10:00.

"I know what!" Robert suddenly said. "Let's go over to the train station and take the train back to Uniondale. It's only one stop, and then we'll walk over to the park and see if there are any ducks we can feed at the pond and play on the playground equipment."

"That's a terrific idea! But what'll we feed the ducks?"

"I'll scrape off my sleeve. Do ducks like meatballs and pepperoni?"

"Sure, they won't turn down a free meal. Let's go."

A half-dark train was standing in the station. Uniondale was one stop away. The whole ride took about a minute and a half.

"Ron?"

"What?"

"Let's stow away. Let's sneak the ride. We'll hide in the john and get off at our stop. It'll be fun."

"Are you kidding? What if they caught us?"

"You know what they do if they catch anyone hitching a ride on a train?" he asked.

"What?"

"They throw them off at the next stop."

"That's all?"

"That's all. Ev and I have done it a million times. Come on. The last car is dark and they won't even see us get on. This time of night, on a Saturday especially, they only have one conductor, and he usually sleeps under his *Daily News*."

We climbed up the steps and boarded the darkened railroad car. Robert took my hand and led me down the empty aisle toward the back of the car where there's always a dirty bathroom. You really have to be bursting your bladder to use one.

We squeezed into the tiny room and Robert closed the door. It smelled awful.

"Hey," I said, "what time's this train supposed to leave, anyway?"

"I don't know!" Robert said and laughed. "I never thought of that."

"Robert, we could be stuck in this john for an hour!"

"Yeah. You don't have a time-table on you, do you?"

"Oh, sure, I always carry a Uniondale time-table. Along with my driver's license and French dictionary."

"Okay. You want to get off?"

I never got to answer because at that moment the train lurched forward and we were moving.

"How's that for timing?" Robert laughed as we were thrown on top of each other by the movement of the train. "*Ow!*"

"What did you hit?" I asked.

"My back. On the sink. Oh! I think I broke something."

"Probably the sink."

"No, really. It hurts when I laugh."

"Turn around." I rubbed his back. "It's just bruised. You'll live. Now get ready, we've got to get off in a minute."

We braced ourselves. Robert opened the door a crack but it was okay. Our car was still dark, with no sign of a conductor or anyone. He motioned me to follow him and we stepped across the little platform that they have between the cars, and stood by the door, ready to get off.

"This is it," Robert said, taking my hand again. "We're pulling into Uniondale. Quick!"

"Quick is right," I said. "We're not stopping."

"Oh my God," he said. "We're not stopping!"

"I thought I just said that."

"Guess what, Ron?"

"What?"

"I forgot this one little thing. If it's not rush hour, the train won't stop at the rinky-dink stations unless they see someone waiting on the platform. Otherwise they go right through. It becomes an express!"

"No, it doesn't! It stops at Lynbrook, that's a transfer point. I used to live there."

"Well," he said, "with my luck we could go clear through to New York. You were right. The night *wasn't* over yet. Who wins, Caroline or Laura . . .?"

The train *did* stop at Lynbrook. We thumbed a ride home with my old friend Sunny Robbins' brother. Last August I had a crush on him. But then we moved away.

∞

"Robert, I had the best time!" I told him.

"Me, too, Ron. I'm sorry about the train."

"I loved it!" I said.

"Next time we'll do something more conventional," he said. "Like a nice safe movie."

"Next time we hitch to Vermont," I said. "G'night."

Chapter 10

On Friday the 30th, I was a basket case. Evelyn said that was a good sign. I didn't think it was a good sign that I had to go to the bathroom every twenty minutes. Both Evelyn and Robert were calm as anything. Robert even said he forgot the church show was that night and made other plans. We both hit him with our book bags until he screamed that he was kidding.

I couldn't eat a thing at dinner and spent about two hours getting dressed. I tried on one T-shirt after another. Evelyn said it should be a perfectly plain shirt to contrast with her ridiculous outfit: a pink tent dress with platform shoes and orange scarf tied around her head. That was okay with me. I wanted to blend in with the scenery. Also I was to wear no make-up. She would wear enough for both of us.

Lenny dropped us off at the church at 7:30, about an hour before the show was supposed to start. Robert was in a great mood because his father wasn't going to be back from his business trip.

The only ones in the hall were Mr. and Mrs.

Farber and their daughters, Karen and Emily. Evelyn introduced me to Karen, the one whose word on local gossip could never be doubted.

The four Farbers were setting up chairs and checking the lighting.

"Hey, we never rehearsed with lighting," Robert said.

"It's all right," Evelyn reassured him, "I already talked to them about it. We'll have a spotlight on us and everything else will be dark. It'll work since we're only going to be in one place except for the entrance and exit. You'll have a piano light." She looked over at the piano. "*Karen!* Where's the piano light?"

"I dunno. *Ma!* Where's the piano light?"

"Look on the piano!" Mrs. Farber yelled from backstage.

"It's not *on* the piano," Karen yelled.

"Well then look *under* the piano!"

"Under the piano?"

Robert looked and sure enough, there was a small lamp with the cord wrapped around its base, directly under the piano.

"Where's the outlet?" Robert wanted to know.

"Where's the outlet, Karen?" Evelyn asked.

"*Ma! Where's the outlet?*"

"*Under the piano!*" Mrs. Farber hollered.

"Evelyn," I said, "guess where you'll find me when they introduce us?"

"Under the piano," she laughed.

But I wasn't. I was where I was supposed to be. Stage left, in the wings, waiting for our turn. We were next to last. I never thought I'd make it, but by the time the show was three quarters over, I was fine. I was even yawning. Evelyn almost fell over her platforms when Mrs. Farber introduced Bonnie Beardsley, who came back from wherever she moved to, for a special appearance with her fire baton. Evelyn said she was glad Robert was somewhere out in the audience because if they saw each other's faces she would have split her seams laughing.

My own favorite was Mrs. Hetrick, Diane's mother, who sang *Mi chiamano Mimi* from the opera "La Boheme." Evelyn said that Mimi was supposed to be this poor fragile, delicate thing, which Mrs. Hetrick sure wasn't and when she hit a high note, all of her chins waggled. Evelyn thought it was beautiful.

"I'll take you to the opera sometime, Ronnie," she said. "You could use a little culture in your life."

"Swell," I told her.

Our turn came after a drum solo by Walter Cress, who was ten years old, and who made the whole stage vibrate. Evelyn's hair, piled up on her head with the scarf over it, moved with each beat, and we were giggling, so that by the time Mrs.

Farber introduced us, "*And na-ow, 'the Three R's in a pantomime of Two Girls at the Movies*'," we were both pretty relaxed.

Robert played *Love Will Keep Us Together* and the spotlight went on when the stage got dark. The spotlight shone on the two chairs we were going to sit in at center stage, so until we got in range of it, the audience couldn't see our entrance, but that was okay. Evelyn entered first, carrying a pretend shopping bag which looked like it was weighing her down, and I followed, just the straight man. Then we made a big show of trying to find the right row to sit in, not too far up front and not too far in the back. I stood still while she pantomimed walking up and down the aisles and peering down the rows. Once she stepped on someone's foot and was supposed to be apologizing while she smacked the person in front of him with her shopping bag. Finally, I dragged her away from that row and found us two seats, which were the ones the spotlight was hitting.

First, we reacted to the movie. We laughed and pointed at the "screen" and then our faces changed together and we began to cry. Then I laughed while she cried and she gave me an elbow in the ribs. All this time, Robert was playing the kind of music they used to play in silent movies—scary chords when the villain is on and tinkly stuff for the happy parts, with a little bit of *Hearts and Flowers* for the sad parts.

After we were settled in, it was time for Evelyn to open her "shopping bag", which was filled with, what else? Food! Robert played *Tea for Two* and Evelyn pretended to take out a big sandwich, and I mean, *big*. She held her arms far apart and her hands open like she was holding a four-foot ear of corn. Then she tried to unwrap it and we both made believe the paper was rustling and disturbing everybody. Finally, Evelyn was so disgusted at the comments she was "hearing" behind her that she stood up, crumpled the "paper" and threw it at someone in back. Then I pretended to be hit on the head, as the "someone" threw it back at Evelyn.

The people were laughing it up and I felt good. I wanted to poke Evelyn and smile at her but I didn't think that's what a real actress would do.

Anyway, then Robert played *Yes, We Have No Bananas* and Evelyn took out a banana which she made a big deal out of peeling, dropped the banana and ducked to watch it roll down through the seats.

By the time we got to the argument with the usher who was going to throw us out, I was having such a good time I didn't want to get off the stage. But finally we heard *Love Will Keep Us Together* and we walked off, being pulled by the make-believe usher. My final bit was to come back on, alone, and pantomime picking up Evelyn's shopping bag, which she had left by mistake, and stagger out under the weight of it.

We got lots and lots of applause. I thought, the

most of any act. Robert stood up at the piano and Evelyn and I both held out our left hands to him so the audience would know who was playing, which of course, they did anyway, but Evelyn said that was the professional thing to do.

When it was all over, Mrs. Farber congratulated us and told us to think of another funny pantomime for the PTA show at Christmas. Evelyn said, "See? I told you!" and all our parents came up to us with big grins on their faces. Robert's mother and two sisters kissed us all and Evelyn's and my mom and dad said how proud they were. Even Lenny said he laughed. A couple of times.

Afterwards all of us, with our families, went to Blaine's, which is this big ice cream place, and we put three tables together and drove the place up the wall with our noise.

It was the happiest night I think I ever had.

Chapter 11

The next morning, Robert and I went over to Evelyn's for breakfast. When we walked into the kitchen, Mrs. Racanelli was standing over the stove, flipping what Evelyn said were one-hundred-and-eighty strawberry pancakes.

"That's about right," Mrs. Racanelli said, looking frazzled. "It sure seems that way! My kids sure love strawberry pancakes . . ."

"Lenny gets fifty-five, Stewart gets fifty-five, *I* get fifty-five, and you two can have the rest," Evelyn said.

"Is she kidding?" I asked Robert.

"Sure she's kidding," Robert answered. "She's not leaving *any* for us two!"

Mrs. Racanelli laughed and plunked down three plates loaded with pancakes. There was strawberry syrup, too.

"Evelyn," she said, "if you want the boys to eat in their room this morning, the least you can do is take their tray up for me."

"Okay," she said. "Be right down!"

"These are *good*, Mrs. Racanelli," I said with my mouth full.

"Thanks, Ronnie, they're one of my specialties," she answered.

Evelyn came back and sat down. She managed to clean up her plate and talk non-stop at the same time.

"I wanted Lenny and Stew upstairs this morning," she began, "so I could talk to you about tonight."

"Yes, Ms. Director . . ." Robert said, smiling.

"No, really, Robert, there are some things you should know . . ."

Evelyn said that according to everything she's ever read about show business, the second night of doing a show is always a let-down. She said it's something to do with the fact that you feel so high and so terrific after doing this thing you've practiced and practiced for so long, especially if the audience loves it, that after that it's bound to be not as good. And she said with us it was probably going to be true, because we had a grownup audience first and now it would be a kid audience.

Robert said she shouldn't have told us that because now we'd be expecting disappointment.

I didn't expect anything. I was feeling wonderful and nothing could spoil it. Mom and Dad were going out for dinner by themselves and I was going to eat at Evelyn's so we could spend all day getting ready for the party. Evelyn had to make the cheese puffs. Skunky was supposed to come over to her house to help, but we also had to make masks for the Halloween part of the party. We all agreed we were too old for costumes but Miss Fisk thought it would be fun to make nutty masks. The idea was to make a mask of the person you wanted to be or the person you thought you were.

Robert decided to be the famous jazz pianist, Oscar Peterson, so he cut out a close-up of Peterson's hand on the keyboard from one of his music magazines. Then he cut holes in two of the black keys for his eyes, tied a piece of thin string on either side, and wore the hands as a mask.

"Why didn't you cut out his *face?*" Evelyn wanted to know. "You look really weird with a pair of hands where your face ought to be!"

"Well, his hands are the most important thing," Robert said. "I mean, that's where his talent is. And that's what I really want—his talent. I don't really want to be Oscar Peterson, the man. I don't even know what kind of life he has. I mean, maybe he's miserable or something."

"That's very far out, Robert," Evelyn said.

Evelyn decided to make a big cork for a mask, put it on and go as a bottle of Mateus wine, but Robert and I talked her out of it, since you were supposed to be a person.

"But I don't know who I wanna be," she wailed.

"You want to be an actress, don't you?" I suggested. "Why don't you go as your favorite actress."

"Yeah, I want to be an actress," she said, "but not like anyone else. I want to be different."

"Well, be someone else for tonight. Pick somebody. How about . . ."

"Cher!" yelled Robert and we all cracked up.

"Can you see me as 'Cher'?" Evelyn roared. "One of my thighs is wider than she is!"

"No," I said, "it has to be an actress. A great one, because you're going to be great. Now think."

We sat down on Evelyn's living room rug and thought.

"What about Katharine Hepburn?" Robert said.

"Too skinny, too," Evelyn answered.

"Oh, stop. It doesn't matter about the weight. Like Robert said, it's the talent," I told her. "How about just making a great big star and wearing that, with your name written on it?"

"Oh, great," she said. "I'll do that. Now, what about you?"

"Yeah, Ron," Robert said.

I pulled a face. "There's nobody I want to be besides me," I told them. "Maybe I should just wear a window pane."

Evelyn said, "You'd better go as the person you think you are, instead of the person you want to be."

"Oh, well, then I'll go as 'Wonder Woman'," I said.

"No, seriously," Evelyn said.

"What do you mean, 'seriously'. Don't you think of me as 'Wonder Woman'?"

"Wonder *Bread*, maybe," Evelyn said, grinning.

"I really don't think of myself as anybody yet," I said. "I don't know what I am now. I think I'll make a big circle and put a question mark in it and wear that."

"That's a good idea," Robert said. "A question mark leaves room for anything."

"Right. That's what I'll do."

∞

The party was fun. None of the older kids showed up and there were mostly seventh and eighth graders there.

Some of the masks were pretty good. Miss Fisk even had one, a big picture of Diana Ross. I thought Miss Fisk was much prettier than Diana Ross.

A couple of kids danced, like Billy Fenner, but most of us were happy listening to the records and kidding around. Bev had set up a haunted house in one part of the room and she really did a good job with it. Even though we knew we were touching spaghetti instead of witches' intestines, it was still yucky and eerie. And Miss Fisk had a huge metal tub with apples in it for bobbing and also some

apples hanging from strings that a boy and girl had
to bob for together.

Robert didn't play piano at all. He stayed with me
until it was time to do the act. We were the only
ones performing. There was supposed to be a rock
group. Mr. Vincent had asked Evelyn if her older
brother would play but Stewart said, "For a bunch
of eighth graders? Forget it." So that was out. Then
there were some ninth graders who were going to
do it but both the bass and guitar players got the
flu, so that didn't work out either.

When we were ready to go on, I wasn't even nervous. We didn't have a spotlight this time, just the
plain room lights, and I guess we were already feeling the let-down that Evelyn told us we would feel.
Karen Farber and Diane Hetrick were there and
they had already seen us the night before so we
didn't expect much of a reception.

We were right. Being able to see everyone's face
distracted me. Billy Fenner kept going back and
forth to the refreshment table. The only real laughing came from Mr. Vincent and Miss Fisk.

Evelyn was disgusted. "That's it!" she said.
"From now on we work only for adult audiences!"

"In the dark," Robert said.

"It's my fault," Evelyn mumbled. "I blew it."

"You did not," I told her. "You were great. It
was just a bad time to do it. And the place wasn't
right . . ."

". . . And the audience. And the lights . . ." she went on.

"And Billy Fenner chewed too loud."

"And Barbara coughed too much."

"And Mr. Vincent and Miss Fisk didn't laugh loudly enough."

"*And we were terrible!*" Evelyn yelled and we started to laugh. Pretty soon we were laughing so hard we couldn't stop. Some other kids started staring at us and giggling because we were holding our stomachs and gulping for air.

Suddenly, Evelyn stopped laughing as quickly as she had started. "Mom!" she cried. "What are you doing here?"

Then Robert and I stopped laughing and turned to see Mrs. Racanelli, looking absolutely white. Her hands were fists, and I remember very well watching her two thumbs rubbing and rubbing against her bent forefingers. I kept watching her fists because in that split second of time when I had looked up at her face, I saw that it was me she was staring at, not Evelyn. Not Robert. She was looking at me and her face was awful.

"Ronnie . . . I came to get you, dear," she began.

"Me? Why?" I was still watching her fists. I couldn't look at her face and I didn't know why.

"Come over here, honey . . ." she took my arm and led me away from the others. Evelyn started to follow, but her mother put up her hand and Evelyn stayed where she was, next to Robert, who hadn't moved. I could hear the noise in the room die down. I wanted it to go on, I didn't want to hear Mrs. Racanelli's voice any more and she hadn't even said anything.

She put her hands on both my shoulders and leaned down. "Ronnie, I've just come from the hospital. There's been an automobile accident . . ."

There was a song I thought of. It began to go through my head. I don't remember what it was.

"Someone sideswiped your father's car on Sunrise Highway . . ."

I thought about my mask with the big question mark . . .

Mrs. Racanelli put her arm tight around my shoulder and began walking me toward the door. "Come on, let's go," she almost whispered. "My car's right out front." She put up her hand again, motioning Robert and Evelyn to stay back. I looked at their faces and they were blank.

"We're going over to the hospital now, honey," I could hear her saying. She opened the door for me on the passenger's side and I sat down. It took a million years for her to walk around to the other side of the car and get in. I didn't care. I wasn't thinking of anything and all I felt was fear.

"We're going to see your mom now," she said. "She's just fine. Just fine."

Mom was fine. I didn't ask any questions. It took twenty-five minutes to get to the hospital. We took the elevator to the second floor where I saw Mom sitting on a couch with some doctor next to her. She looked up and saw me and that's when she started to cry. And that's when I knew I was right about the things I was feeling when I first saw Mrs. Racanelli's face at the "Y."

Mom held onto me and cried.

"Your mom and dad were coming home from the restaurant," Mrs. Racanelli was saying. "Another car . . . coming from the other direction . . . just went out of control . . ."

Her voice sounded like one tone. Like a buzz in my ear.

"It just rammed into your parents' car . . . on the driver's side . . ." she touched my shoulder . . . "your mom was the only passenger. She didn't get a scratch. But . . . the drivers of both cars . . ."

Buzzzzzzz.

". . . were killed instantly . . . Ronnie, it wasn't your father's fault . . ."

Chapter 12

Miss Fisk hugged me at the funeral. Seeing her there made me want to cry. I thought it was very strange that seeing Miss Fisk at my father's funeral would make me want to cry, since I hadn't cried at all before.

There were a lot of relatives . . . and friends from Lynbrook. I saw Sunny Robbins . . .

Robert held my hand very tightly when he came in before the ceremony. I think he was with his mother. I looked for him when it was over but it was so crowded I never found him. Evelyn was there . . .

I fell asleep during the ceremony. Nobody knew it because my head was down and I was only out for a few minutes, but my eyes were too heavy, I couldn't keep them open. I didn't even feel badly about it until later.

When the funeral was over, we went home. Mom and me, and aunts and uncles. There was a lot of food but only some of the aunts and uncles ate any. Mostly we just sat.

I still hadn't cried.

"Such a brave girl, she didn't even cry," Daddy had said that time I fell off my tricycle. Was it because I was brave that I didn't cry? I kept seeing that mask, that big circle with the question mark. It filled up a big space in my head.

"A boy left this for you at the door, Ronnie," a lady said. Aunt Lyddie. She handed me a flat package, wrapped in tissue paper.

It was the picture from Robert's room, the one he'd had since he was little. The one I'd liked so much.

And there was a letter with it. A poem.

Pain.
It has a pattern.
First it's too terrible to think about
So you close the door on it.
It won't stay out.
It pounds and pounds until you let it in
And then it crushes you.
It winds around your head and throat
Until you can't cry another tear
Or rip another pillow case
And then it moves from the front of your mind
To the back.
That's where it stays
And it becomes like your clothes or your comb:
You don't think about it
Until you need it.

Then I remember hearing someone cry. The noises were so awful, so choked and hard that I wanted to make it stop but I couldn't. I don't know when I realized it was me.

Moody Blues

Chapter 13

For the next couple of days it was like we were suspended in space somewhere, Mom and me. Some people came over—aunts, friends—I remember Mrs. Racanelli was there once . . .

I stayed very close to Mom. Lots of times it seemed as if she didn't know I was even there. Then other times, she would suddenly grab me and hold onto me very tightly. Sometimes she cried a lot and other times she just sat, staring at nothing.

I remember mealtimes because Aunt Lydia would always be either pushing us to the table or putting plates on our laps. That was how I realized the day was passing, by the meals. I really don't remember thinking very much. It was like when your arm falls asleep and you don't feel it at all.

Monday night, Mom screamed in her sleep. The doctor had given us both pills and I was so groggy that at first I didn't know where I was. I thought the sounds I was hearing were part of my dream, but the moaning didn't stop and I finally woke up. When I realized it was Mom and what was happening, I got right out of bed. But I guess I was still dizzy from the pill or something, because I fell down. I ended up practically crawling into Mom's room.

The light was on and she wasn't sleeping any more. She was lying on her stomach, rolling around the bed, and she didn't know I was there. It hurt me so much to see her that way—and kind of shocked me, too. I felt for a minute as if I were the mother and she were the child who'd had a nightmare.

I started shivering because I was cold and still half-asleep, so I figured the best thing to do was get in bed with Mom and maybe she'd feel better knowing I was there.

I pulled up the covers that were half on the floor and got under them. As soon as she knew I was in the room, she stopped moaning and sat up, reaching for the tissues. I handed her the box.

She said in a hoarse voice, "Oh. Baby. I'm sorry I woke you."

"It's okay," I said. "You should have come in if you were awake."

"I really didn't want to disturb you," she said. "I just can't . . . I mean, I can't get hold of myself."

"It just happened, Mom," I told her, feeling about ninety years old suddenly. "It's too soon to worry about getting hold of yourself. You will."

"You seem to be all right . . ." she said.

I felt awful when she said that. As if I didn't feel sorry enough. I couldn't explain how I felt. Just . . . numb. So I didn't say anything.

"You know, Ronnie . . . We were so close . . . I can't get it through my head that I'll never see him again. That's what I find so hard to believe." She banged both her fists on the bed.

And we just sat there.

"I love you, baby. You're all I have now. We're all each other has," she said after a while.

"I love you, too, Mom," I said. "Do you want me to stay here tonight?"

"Yes. No. I . . . I don't know."

So I just stayed there. I sat with my back pushed against the wall because I didn't want to fall asleep while Mom was still awake.

I fell asleep sitting up.

∞

Tuesday morning my back hurt. Mom was still sleeping. And the idea in my head was what I had fallen asleep thinking: that for a time, I would kind of be taking care of Mom. She'd be all right soon, painting and everything. She was strong, I knew she was a strong person. She had always encouraged me to be strong, too, and independent. Women are independent these days, she'd tell me, and your generation will be even more so!

I went to the kitchen and put on some coffee. I had never done it before, so the first time, when it quit perking and I poured a cup, it looked like tea. So I put in more coffee and less water and it came out looking like mud. I wondered if I should have saved the tea-like stuff to mix with the mud-like stuff and then maybe it would be right. Finally I gave up, found some instant and just boiled water, so it would be nice and hot for Mom.

Then I went into my room to find something to do. I didn't want to doze off, I wanted to be up and around when Mom got out of bed.

I picked up a *New York* magazine and started to read about a place that serves the best chili on the West Side, when I heard her moving around. I ran into her bedroom. She was just putting on her robe. She looked like a ghost with two black eyes.

"Hi. Coffee's ready. Do you care if it's instant?"

"Hi, honey," she said. "Are you okay? I'm sorry about . . . waking you last night. You went back to your own room, didn't you?"

"No, no. I stayed with you. I just got up first," I said. "Come have something to eat."

She sagged back onto the bed. "I don't think I want anything now. Thanks."

"Please, Mom . . . Have something . . ."

"Ronnie, just let me sit here for a while," she said.

"Hey, I'll make you anything you want. You just tell me what to do."

"I said I don't want anything now!" she snapped. Then she got up and hugged me. "I'm sorry, I'm sorry," she kept saying, smoothing my hair. "All right, I'll have some coffee."

∞

"Hello, Ronnie?"

"Yeah. Hi, Evelyn."

"Hi. I just . . . I thought I'd call . . . I mean, I just called to say 'hello'."

"Well, that was nice of you."

"My mother wants to know if you need anything."

"No. Thanks. My Aunt Lyddie came over Monday and yesterday and she brought dinner. She'll probably show up the rest of the week."

"How is your . . . um . . . Do you think you'll be coming back to school soon?"

"Probably next week."

"That'll be good. It'll probably take your mind off . . . everything. For a while, I mean."

"Yeah."

"Well . . . I'll call you . . ."

"Good. So long."

∞

"Ron? Hi."

"Hi, Robert. Thanks for sending . . . you know."

"Oh. You're welcome."

"It really . . . meant a lot to me."

"Good. I tried to imagine how you were feeling inside."

"Evelyn just called a while ago."

"Oh, she did? I would have called before, but I

thought you maybe needed some time alone with your mother and everything."

"I guess so. Mostly I've been sleeping."

"Did the doctor give you something?"

"Only Sunday and Monday. Nothing yesterday or today. My mother is still taking some pills, though. How's school?"

"The same. When will you be back?"

"I guess Monday."

"Is it okay if I call again before that?"

"Sure."

"Okay, then, I will. Take care."

" 'Bye."

∞

"Hello, Ronnie? Evelyn."

"I know. Hi."

"Robert was just here. I told him I was going to call you but he didn't wait. He said he was going to call you from his house."

"Okay. How're you doing?"

"Fine. How are *you* doing?"

"All right, I guess."

"Listen, you won't believe this—Miss Fisk finally got me up on a rope today! I got two inches off the floor. Everyone cheered, it was a riot! Oh, hey, I'm sorry. I mean . . ."

"It's okay, Evelyn. Really. I'm glad you got up on the rope. I'll have to see that when I come back."

"Right. Well . . . talk to you."

"Uh huh. 'Bye."

∞

"Ron?"

"Hi, Robert."

"I just left Evelyn's. We really miss you at school. How's your mother?"

"Not too good."

"Yeah. Well, maybe I shouldn't come over then. I was going to ask you if I could . . ."

"I'd really like you to come over. But maybe we better wait until the weekend. Today's Thursday . . . it'll probably be all right by Saturday. I feel . . . I don't know. Mom has Aunt Lyddie and Aunt Ruth to talk to and I just . . . I feel very strange. Every time it gets to be around 6:00, I know the commuter train's coming in and I keep expecting . . ."

"Yeah. I know."

"Did your father get back from his business trip yet?"

"No, tomorrow night."

"It's weird the way things happen, isn't it?"

"It sure is."

"Well, I'd better check on my mother. She was asleep, but I think I hear her getting up."

"Okay. Maybe I'll see you Saturday. I'll call you tomorrow."

∞

Robert came over Saturday and I was glad, because the house was full of relatives—uncles who hadn't come over with their wives during the week, and some people who hadn't been able to get here in time for the funeral. Robert and I went into my room, and except for a few aunts who thought it was their duty to pat me on the head, they mostly left us alone.

"They all say the same thing," I told Robert.

"They don't know what to say," he answered. "They know they can't help you so they just say stuff they think they're supposed to say. Evelyn's like that."

"I try to make her feel comfortable when she calls," I said, "But I guess I wouldn't know how to behave either. I don't know how to behave *now*."

He looked at the wall over my bed. "I see you put up the picture."

"Right away. It's a sad picture, but it makes me feel better to look at it. How's your father?"

"He's in a good mood. His trip went well."

"How's he treating you?"

"He's not. That's how I know he's in a good mood."

"Gee, Robert, I wish you'd play the piano. Is that a terrible thing to say?"

"No. There's nothing terrible about music. I'd like to play for you, but some people might think it was, you know, entertaining at a sad time."

"But a person needs that," I blurted out. "There's been so much misery here—it seems like a year! I can't stand it any more!"

He sat up from a slouching position on my bed. "Listen," he said. "You're right. Nobody can stay miserable for that long a stretch. You need a break from that like you need a break from work. Don't feel like you're committing a sin."

I looked at him. That's just how I felt.

"Y'know, he went on, some really awful stuff has gone down at my house. No kidding. And all of us, my mother and Caroline and Laurie and me, we could be depressed all the time if we let ourselves. When we can't stand it, we kid it. It's not a sin to try to make yourself feel better, Ron."

I started to cry. I didn't want to, in front of him.

"You're alive, remember," he said.

Chapter 14

Sunday night I took out the ironing board to iron my blue-checked shirt for school the next day. The laundry had been piling up and Aunt Ruth finally put it through the machines but she hadn't ironed anything. I thought that there probably were some of my father's things in the laundry but I guess Aunt Ruth took care of them because I didn't see them in the basket. I didn't think I could stand to see them.

"What are you doing?" Mom asked.

"Getting my stuff ready for school," I answered.

"You're going to school tomorrow? So soon?"

I didn't know what to say. Was it too soon?

"Well . . . I thought . . . It's been a week, I thought I'd better go back. I . . . I've missed a lot."

"No, honey, of course you should go back," she said. "I'm sorry, I was just . . . You go to school tomorrow." She nodded. She looked a lot better, I thought. "I'll help you with the iron," she said, putting in water for the steam.

She stayed with me while I ironed, sitting on the kitchen stool.

"What will you do tomorrow?" I asked.

She smiled a little. "I haven't given it one single thought," she answered. "I guess I could go shopping. I don't even know what's in the house . . . what we're out of or anything. I guess the laundry's taken care of . . ."

"Aunt Lyd coming tomorrow?" I asked.

"I don't know. Maybe."

"Why don't you paint?" I asked carefully.

"Paint?" she asked, like she never heard the word. "Oh. Well . . ."

∞

My alarm went off at 6:30 and I was wide awake. For the first time since the accident I began to feel I could look forward to something and it felt good. I remembered what Robert said. He was right, I was alive. I didn't die, too. And that didn't mean I didn't love my father.

I got dressed quickly and went into the kitchen to get breakfast for myself. There were a few things I did know how to do in the kitchen, like how much milk to pour in a bowl of Froot Loops, how to stir the orange juice so it didn't come out in layers, and how to push down the toaster. I had just done all that when Mom came in.

"You didn't have to get up," I told her.

"Ronnie?" she said. She sounded like she was about to cry.

"What?" I said, feeling scared again.

"Ronnie, please?"

"Please, what?" I said, going over to her.

"Stay home another day," she said.

No, I thought. *No, I don't want to. Don't make me.* But I didn't say anything.

"Just another day, please, Ronnie," she begged. "I thought last night I could handle it, but I can't, I just can't. I'll be okay tomorrow, but please, honey, just one more day." And she did cry, plopping down at the table with her head on her arms.

I knelt next to her. "Okay, Mom. Don't cry, it's okay. I'll stay home today. I will, don't worry."

At noon, Robert called from Harry's to find out why I wasn't in school. I told him Mom felt better with me home another day and I was sure I'd be back Tuesday.

I spent the morning wandering around. I thought of turning on the TV but I really didn't feel like it. Aunt Lyddie arrived at about three with a casserole. She put it in the refrigerator and then sat down on the couch next to Mom.

"Dot? Have you thought about what you're going to do? I mean, are you going to stay here in the house? Fred and I were wondering if you might be happier coming back to Lynbrook where we can all look after you and Ronnie."

I closed my eyes.

"I haven't thought, Lydia," Mom said. "I haven't thought about anything . . . I don't want to think about anything."

"Well . . . you're right, dear, you're right," Aunt Lyddie said, patting Mom's knee. "But later on, consider it. We're all worried about you."

I wanted to scream: Do I have to lose *everything?*

As soon as Aunt Lyd left, I said to Mom, "You know, we never got all our unpacking done. From the move. Why don't we spend the rest of the day and get some of our stuff out of boxes? There isn't that much left and we could probably finish it all."

"What for?" Mom said blankly.

Because it's something to do! I thought. *Because I want to know we're going to stay here! Because I'm starting to go crazy.* But I didn't yell. I said, very quietly, "Because we haven't done anything at all for over a week and I think we should do something so we don't have to think any more."

"Yes," Mom said. "You're right. But I don't want to."

I took her hand and led her into the den. There were Daddy's shelves on the wall . . . He'd had such a good time building them . . . But there weren't very many books up yet. We had only unpacked one book box and there were two more big ones to go.

"Let's do the books, Mom," I said.

She looked at the shelves and I thought she would cry, but she didn't. She just looked very tired. Slowly, we started to unpack books. For a second it seemed like I was outside my own body, watching myself. I thought we looked like two wind-up toys, Mom and me. Taking out books, putting them on shelves, going back for more. Something to do.

"This box doesn't have books in it," I said, opening the third box.

"What?"

"This box," I said. "It's got broken dishes in it. And potato peelings!"

"What?" Mom looked up for the first time, and came over to peer in the box. "Oh, my God, the moving men packed our garbage!" she said.

"How could they do that?" I poked around some more in the box. An old detergent carton, an empty meat package—it smelled awful. "They did! They packed our garbage! That's funny!" I started to laugh, then quickly put my hand over my mouth. Mom looked at me and frowned. Then her eyes got dull again.

"I'll take the box outside," I said.

When I came back, Mom was sitting on a footstool, crying. She was holding a book of Picasso prints Dad had given her for their anniversary right before we moved.

She held the book close. "The last time . . . we all unpacked together. It was something we did— together," she said through the tears.

"I know," I said, beginning to cry with her. "But now we have to do it alone."

∞

Robert called every day for the rest of the week to find out why I wasn't back in school. I didn't know what to tell him. I was ready each night to set my alarm but at the last minute, Mom begged me to stay home one more day. Robert kept offering to collect all the work I'd missed and bring it over but for some reason I thought it might upset Mom so I told him not to.

By Thursday afternoon I was so jittery I went out for a walk. The air felt good. It was beginning to get cold. I went around the block twice, and the whole time I thought about Mom. I figured it would be a good thing if she started to paint again. Before the . . . before this, she never missed a day, not even when she wasn't feeling well.

I came home and suggested it to her. She didn't say anything, so I went into the studio and set up her easel and put the paints on her palette. I knew just how to do it, in which order she liked them. Then I went back into the kitchen where she was staring into space over a cold cup of coffee and handed her her smock.

"No," she said. "Put it away."

"Everything's ready," I told her. "I've done your palette and set up the easel. Go play."

"Ronnie, no!"

"Mom, you have to—"

"Sit here with me," she said. "Talk to me."

Chapter 15

All the kids from the bus pushed past me. Staring at the school, I thought, *the last time I saw this building my father was alive.* I figured it was going to be like that for a long time. I'd remember the last Thanksgiving . . . the last Christmas . . . the last snowfall . . .

I was glad I had a lot of schoolwork to make up. Sometimes, when I really listened to my teachers I didn't think about anything except the classwork and it was a big relief.

When Gym came, eighth period, I was really looking forward to seeing Miss Fisk.

"Hi, honey, it's good to see you," was all she said in the locker room and that made me feel another kind of relief.

"Are we having rope-climbing today?" I asked her.

"Shh!" from Evelyn, changing her clothes.

"We sure are!" Miss Fisk grinned. "You can't stop once you've got the momentum going, right, Evelyn?"

"Oh, right, right," Evelyn grumbled. "Wait'll

you see this, Ronnie, I look like a yo-yo going up the string in triple slow motion."

"Wouldn't miss it for the world," I said.

When we got on line after calisthenics, Evelyn didn't move around. She stayed right behind Alice Marie McLaren until she reached the head of the line. I stayed three girls behind, so I'd have enough time to watch her before it was my turn.

"You'll recognize me" Evelyn said, "I'll be the only one sweating *before* I exert myself!"

She was right. Perspiration was running down her cheeks as she gripped the rope. You could really see it. I pushed her with my mind. All my toes were curled inside my sneakers and I put both my thumbs behind my front teeth and pushed as hard as I could.

Come on, *Evelyn!* I whispered in my head, like a silent cheerleader.

Then one of her legs was off the ground. Then both! She was grunting and straining like crazy.

"I'm . . . gonna . . . pull this rope right . . . out of . . . the ceiling!" she said, through her clenched teeth.

"Don't talk, Evelyn, you're doing just great!" Miss Fisk cried. "Keep going, keep going!"

She actually did get halfway up the rope and then just hung there, panting.

"That's . . . as far as I go," she said.

"Fine. Come on down. That was terrific!" Miss

Fisk applauded and so did all the other girls. Evelyn was smiling as she let herself down.

"What'd you think of that!" she said, coming toward me. "When I get up to the top of that thing, you're gonna think King Kong was mashed potatoes! You should have seen me last week. Miss Fisk and Gwenny, you know the girl with the red hair, and Barbara were underneath me, trying to give me a boost. It took all three of them to even get me off the ground," she started to giggle. "And then Barbara said she thought I broke her collar bone!"

I cracked up. It had been so long since I laughed. And I didn't remember that until my side hurt, and then I thought of the night of the show, when the three of us had laughed so hard over something so silly. It seemed like a million years ago. I stopped laughing immediately.

"Oh, Ronnie . . ." Evelyn said, serious, too.

"It's okay, Evelyn. It's okay. I'm allowed to laugh. I can't not laugh for the rest of my life. My daddy would never want that. Because I know it has nothing to do with missing him."

"Ronnie? Everyone's gone ahead of you," Miss Fisk called. "It's your turn."

When Gym was over, Evelyn said, "How about coming over this afternoon? Robert'll come and we'll just sit around and relax. And eat."

I told her I'd just have to make it another time. That morning, when I left for school, Mom was sitting at the kitchen table. She tried to smile and tell me to have a good day, but she didn't quite make it. And she could hardly look at me. I called her at lunch and she sounded awful. So I figured I'd better go straight home.

∞

"Our lawyer was here this afternoon," Mom said when I got in.

"What for?"

"Oh, to talk about . . . insurance and things. I hardly even listened. I knew what he was going to say. Your father and I planned it all together. The point is, money won't be a problem for us right now . . ."

I nodded.

"Anyway," she continued, "I talked to him about maybe selling the house . . . Going back to Lynbrook . . ."

I took a deep breath.

"He said he didn't think it was a good idea to make any decisions when we're under such a strain . . . I thought he was right, don't you?"

"Yes," I said, breathing again.

"Besides, you really like it here, don't you?"

"Yes."

"Then that's what we'll do, we'll stay for a while and see what happens."

I slammed into my room. I didn't want to upset Mom, but in a way I *did* want to upset her. Maybe it was the words "for a while" that bothered me. I threw myself on the bed. My *mother* was what was bothering me and that made me feel just awful.

∝

School let out at noon the day before Thanksgiving. I woke up feeling crummy and stayed feeling crummy. I wanted to keep going to school, I really felt better when I was doing work and seeing the kids. Especially Robert. It was hard to see him on weekends now, so the only time I got to be with him was in school.

Evelyn and Robert and I decided to have lunch at Harry's. It wasn't crowded since most of the school split at noon and went home or wherever.

"Let's have a Thanksgiving party Friday night!" Evelyn said. "We're gonna have so much food left over. We always do, we make enough to feed the population of Arkansas. Come on, let's do it! Nobody'll even have to bring anything."

"Good idea!" Robert said. "After our usual Thanksgiving celebration, I could use a happy event. How about it, Ron?"

"It's a good idea," I said, "but I can't go. Thanks anyway."

"Why not?"

"We're just not ready to celebrate anything yet," I said.

"It would probably be good for you," Robert said quietly.

"Maybe, but I can't. I just can't."

∞

We went to Aunt Lyddie's for Thanksgiving dinner. Uncle Fred had to come over and drag Mom out of the house, but we went. It was very quiet and nobody ate much.

∞

The next thing we had to get through was Christmas. It was extra hard because so many things were happening and I started to really miss not doing them. We had a snow day once when school was closed, and Beverly organized a sleigh-riding party in the park. And the "Y" had a couple of parties and meetings I missed . . .

∞

Helen was having a Christmas party. She sent out great invitations, with each of the kids' faces pasted on a Christmas tree, like they were decorations. She got the pictures by sneaking around the halls in school with a camera. Robert was yawning in his picture. I decided I'd go to that party.

I showed Mom the invitation and she smiled. "Clever," she said.

"I'm gonna call Helen and tell her I'll go, okay?" I said, going to the phone.

"You're going to go?"

"Yeah. I'd like to."

Mom didn't say anything, she just turned and walked into the kitchen.

I followed her.

"Mom? Is it okay?"

"If you want to go, then go," she said.

So I didn't go to that one either.

∞

I spent the first week of Christmas vacation sitting with a set of water colors and a glass of water, drawing black circles and squares on my glass-top desk. I would wipe them off with a paper towel and do them again. It was weird how quickly the hours seemed to go while I smeared that glass with black streaks and blobs.

My mother came in and saw me. Once. She didn't speak, but she stood behind me for a long time and watched. I never looked at her, just pushed that brush around the glass, and felt better when she walked out.

The funny thing is, I didn't know she had left the house, I was so into smearing that paint. And besides, she hardly ever left the house, at least when I was around. But she had, because she came into my room with her coat on and a white box with holes in it in her hand. She sat down on my bed and I put down the brush.

"Hi," she said. The box was now on her lap and something was making a scratching sound.

"Hi," I said. "You went out?"

"Yep. Listen, I . . . I know this vacation hasn't been any . . . fun for you . . . We haven't done anything about Christmas . . . and I can't, Ronnie, I just can't. But I did get something for you . . ."

Scratch, scratch from the box.

"It'll be something for you to do, too. Teaching it to talk."

"Teaching what to talk?"

Mom opened the box and held it out to me with her fingers spread over the top. Crouched inside was a bird. It was gray, with white on its wings, and a crest on top of its head. The crest was yellow. And on each side of its face, two orange spots—like red cheeks.

"Oh, wow!" I said. "He's beautiful! What kind of bird is he?"

"He's a cockatiel," Mom said. "He can learn to talk and whistle . . . Come on, the cage is in the living room."

It was a big cage, and there was a stand to go with it. Mom showed me what the pet shop lady said about putting a paper towel in the bottom and sprinkling some gravel on it for the bird to chew on. There were two dishes in the sides of the cage, one for water and one for food. Mom went out to the car and brought in two bags: one had sunflower seeds and the other a mixture of tiny seeds—hemp, oats and wheat. And there were vitamin drops to put in the water every day.

I hugged her. "Thanks, Mom! I love him!"

"What are you going to call him?"

I looked at the bird, now in the cage, but still crouched—this time in the corner under one of the wooden sticks he was supposed to sit on. "Arthur," I said.

"Arthur? Why Arthur?"

"He looks like an Arthur."

"You're right," she answered. "He definitely does."

"How do you teach him to talk?"

"You have to finger-train him first," Mom said. She explained how you have to get a bird's confidence. He has to feel safe with you and when he does, he'll sit on your finger. Then you have to bring him right up to your lips and teach him one word by saying it over and over very slowly and in a high voice. They hear high voices better than low ones.

"First you have to put your hands all over the cage so he gets used to seeing them. Don't try to touch him at first. Just talk quietly to him and keep your hands where he can see them," Mom told me. "Start with something simple, like 'pretty boy'."

I began right away. For the first fifteen minutes, Arthur stayed scrunched in the corner, but then he crawled out, got up on the stick and started to crack and eat sunflower seeds. It was terrific how he did it with his beak.

The phone rang and I heard Mom answer it.

"Hello? Hello, Robert. I think she's kind of busy right now. Wait a minute and I'll see . . ."

I was standing next to her grabbing the phone while she was saying, "Wait a minute."

"Robert? Wait'll you see what I got!" Mom was shaking her head.

I frowned and put my hand over the phone. "Can't he come over and see Arthur?"

"No, it's too close to dinner. He'll see him another time."

"How about *after* dinner?"

Mom sighed. "All right. But not too late, Ronnie."

∞

Robert loved Arthur. The two of us spent almost an hour with our hands on the cage squeaking "pretty boy" at him. Then Robert whistled a long high note. The bird whistled a short note back. Robert whistled, the bird did. We both started to laugh.

"Teach him a song!" I cried.

Robert slowly whistled the first two notes of *Twinkle, Twinkle, Little Star.* The bird whistled back the notes of the first "Twinkle." In the same key!

"This bird is talented," Robert said. "Send him to school."

"No, it's you," I told him. "You're a good teacher."

"Tell me that after he pecks out *Love Will Keep Us Together* on the piano!" Robert said.

"And uses the pedal at the same time," I answered.

"Wait'll you see what I got you for Christmas," Robert said, and smiled.

Oh, God, I thought, *I didn't get anything for him. For anybody. Okay, it's only Thursday. Christmas is Sunday, I can get something tomorrow.*

"What is it?" I asked him.

"Well, I'm sure not gonna tell you," he said. "But I'll give you a hint: You can't eat it."

"That's a giveaway," I said. "I know what it is. A vacuum cleaner."

"Damn!" Robert said. "I shouldn't have given you that big a hint."

∞

It was a gold I.D. bracelet, with a skinny chain and a skinny gold bar that had my name on it: RON. It was gorgeous.

I got him two Oscar Peterson records, and Mom a small set of acrylic paints. She had never tried acrylics, only oils, and I thought maybe it would get her interested in working again. Before, she had once talked about having a one-woman show.

She smiled at the paints and she thanked me, but she put them away.

∞

We went to Aunt Lyddie's for Christmas dinner. This time, Mom didn't need Uncle Fred to drag her, but she wasn't thrilled about going, either. Aunt Lyd and Uncle Fred had a Christmas tree, but it was table-size, not like their usual bent-over-against-the-ceiling tree. Mom didn't look at it.

Between dinner and dessert, Aunt Lyddie said, "Dot, how about moving back here? To Lynbrook. Have you thought any more about it?"

Mom sighed.

"Because if you have, I'd like to start looking for a place for you . . ."

"Lydia, I'm not making any changes in my life right now. I told you . . ."

Aunt Lyddie dropped that subject, thank God, and went on to a better one.

"You know, Dot, except for coming here today and Thanksgiving, you haven't been out of your house. Haven't seen anyone . . . Haven't even taken poor Ronnie to a movie."

"I'm not . . ."

"*Don't* tell me you're not ready!" Aunt Lyd said firmly. "You'll never be ready unless you start. Are you letting Ronnie see her friends?"

I quickly looked down and began making soup out of my ice cream and fudge sauce.

"I'm not stopping Ronnie from seeing her friends. She sees them. But she likes to keep me company."

"*I'll* keep you company, Dot, and so will Ruth, and Claudia Hornblower and Marge Robbins, and just about—"

"O-kay, Lydia, I get the message, now please let me do things in my own good time."

Silence.

∞

Diane Hetrick was having a New Year's Eve party, but she didn't invite me. Robert said it was because she knew I wouldn't come anyway, otherwise she would have.

"*Can* you come?" he asked. "Diane would love it if you could. She told Evelyn she didn't want to make you feel bad by having to refuse another invitation."

It seemed kind of a weird reason to me. What I thought was, *Diane figured I'd be a downer at her party.*

"Can't go out yet, Robert," I mumbled.

"Well, I'm not going either."

"You're not going? Why?"

"I don't feel like it. How about if I came over to stay with you?"

I dug a pencil point into the wall paneling, broke the pencil and scarred the wall. "No. Thanks. My mother would be . . . left out. I'd better be with her, just the two of us."

"Well, everyone's going out here. Even Laurie, she's staying overnight with one of her girlfriends. I'll be alone. Why don't I call you? We could talk on the phone."

"Don't stay home from the party because of me."

"Look, Ron, I get invited to these parties for two reasons: I'm Evelyn's friend and I can play *The Hustle,* all the Christmas carols and *Auld Lang Syne* on the piano. Believe me, those are the only reasons. I was never a fit-into-the-crowd person."

"Everyone likes you," I told him.

"Yeah, everyone likes Rosey. And if I smashed a hand tomorrow my popularity would fly off into the sunset like 'the wings of man'. I have a good time when I'm with you, and if I can't be with you then I'd rather talk to you on the phone than do my number for Diane Hetrick."

"Okay."

"Okay."

∞

Robert called at exactly 8:00 on New Year's Eve. Mom was lying down on the couch in the den with her eyes closed. She was already in her nightgown. The TV was on.

"Who is it?" she mumbled.

"It's for me, Mom. It's Robert. Go back to sleep," I said.

"Mmmmmph," she said and closed her eyes again.

"This New Year's is getting off to a good start. Everybody's out of the house," Robert said.

"Where'd they go?"

"My parents went to a party given by someone in my father's company. They don't know him too well."

"What do you mean?" I asked.

"He's never invited to a party at the same house twice."

"Why not?"

"Parties do him in. He can't handle booze."

"What happens?"

"You know how he is normally? Well, he's twice that when he's drunk. Oooh, he's a *mean* drunk!"

God, I thought. "What does your mother do?"

"She tries to sit on his mouth. Ahh, she just hopes each time she can get him to stop after one or two. We always give her rabbits' feet and magic charms when they go out. She pours water into his drink and sometimes that works. Anyway, that's enough about 'Life with the Roses', brought to you by Ivory Snow, for softer undies. How are things there?"

"Quiet. My mother's sleeping on the couch in the den. Arthur's wide awake, though. You should hear him, he's whistling 'Twinkle'."

"Twinkle, Twinkle, Little Star?"

"No, just 'Twinkle'. That's all you taught him so far."

"He's bright, but no initiative," Robert said. "No get-up-and-go. He'll never make it. Jeez, I sound like my father!"

"Let's play 'Name That Song'," I suggested. "I'll give you a hint, and you guess how many notes it'll take you to guess the tune. Then I'll hum the notes."

It was fun and we played for half an hour.

After that, we talked about Mr. Vincent and Miss Fisk. Robert brought it up.

"You heard about the vigilante committee?" he asked.

"The what?"

"Oh, the bridge club my mother belongs to. She was telling Caroline and me about some of the things they're saying. She was pretty upset."

"Who? What are they saying?" I asked.

"You know, Mrs. Farber, Mrs. Hetrick, and some of those others. They want Fisk and Vincent transferred to another school. Two separate schools, as a matter of fact."

"You're kidding. Because of the color thing?"

"Sure! Couple of years ago, two teachers met in school and got married and nobody said anything. The PTA even gave them a party. But they were both *white*."

"But it's none of anybody's business," I said.

"You know that and I know that but someone ought to tell the vigilante committee," he answered.

"Why do awful things always happen to nice people?" I said.

"I don't know the answer to that," he said. "I'll work on it."

The subject was depressing us, so we talked about other things—Evelyn; Robert's failing science due to broken experiments; which was better for pimples, rubbing alcohol or Clearasil; the possibility of a woman President and who it should be; which was better to listen to while doing homework, funky blues or classical music; whether Marie Osmond was prettier than Donny; how many children did we want to have and what their names would be, all twelve of them; and what it was like to be miserable on New Year's Eve when the rest of the world was having a blast. Except we weren't miserable any more. And it was twelve o'clock.

"Ronnie?"

I whispered "Just a sec" to Robert and covered the mouthpiece with my hand.

"Mom? I'm here . . ."

"What are you doing?" she asked.

"I'm on the phone. It's okay. Rest."

"You're *still* on the phone? What time is it?" Her voice wasn't sleepy any more.

"Twelve."

She was on her feet and in the kitchen instantly. "You have been talking to that boy for *four hours!*"

"Yeah, I guess so," I said. "I wasn't watching the time."

"Hang *up!*" she ordered.

"Okay, let me just wish him a happy new year . . . It's 12:00 . . ."

"I said hang up!"

"Robert, I have to go."

"Do you think we'll be in the Guinness Book of Records for the world's longest phone call?" he asked.

"Let's send it in and see," I said.

"I'm willing to go on for the record if we don't make it."

"Me, too."

"Hang up that phone!" Mom yelled.

I did after I whispered goodbye.

I didn't even look at Mom, I just headed right for my room.

"Ronnie!"

I decided I'd better look at her. "What?"

"From now on I want you to limit your phone conversations to ten minutes."

"Ten minutes!"

"I think you can say all you have to say in ten minutes. It's not as if you don't see your friends every day at school." She didn't sound mad any more, she just sounded tired. But I was mad.

"That's not fair!" I yelled. "You're not being fair. I've tried . . . I've been trying to take care of you, I did everything I could. I wanted to keep busy and do things but I stayed home when you wanted me to . . ." I could feel myself beginning to cry. ". . . And I thought after a while you'd want to be busy, too, and get back to what you *were*. But you're not even trying, you're just picking on *me* . . ." I stopped myself just short of saying: Daddy wouldn't even recognize you now, he wouldn't even understand you now! But I didn't say that, at least I didn't say that.

Mom opened her mouth and tried to say something, so I didn't leave right away. I gave her a chance to get it together, but she ended up not saying whatever it was. She just stood there in her nightgown, put her face in her hands, and cried.

Happy New Year, everybody.

Chapter 16

"What do you mean, only ten minutes?" Evelyn wanted to know the first day of school. "Two of Karen Farber's rumors are good for at least twenty each!"

"Ten minutes, wow," Robert said. "It takes that long to get into a conversation."

"I know," I said.

"What's she gonna do, put on her kitchen timer when the phone rings?"

"I don't know." I was miserable.

∞

Robert called after school that afternoon. He wanted to discuss the Social Studies homework assignment, which was to draw a comic strip frame illustrating one amendment of the Bill of Rights. I had picked Freedom of Worship, and was going to draw a picture of some blacks being barred from entering a white church. Robert was wondering if, for Freedom of the Press, he could get away with drawing Snoopy being arrested for delivering copies of a newspaper. We were just getting around to how to make that clearer when Mom tapped me on the shoulder and told me my ten minutes were up. I wanted to say, "I'll signal when ready," but I didn't.

"I have to go, my ten minutes are up," I told Robert.

"But wait a minute," he said, "I wanted to ask if we could go out on Saturday . . ." Mom was glaring at me.

"Listen, I . . . I have to go."

"I'll call you back!" he yelled.

"No, you better not. 'Bye." I hung up. Five minutes later the phone rang. I raced for it, but Mom got it.

"It's for you," Mom said. "Ten minutes."

"Hello, Ronnie?" It was a strange girl's voice.

"Yes?"

"This is Laurie Rose. Hold on a minute . . ."

"Hi, it's me." Robert.

"Hi!"

"Don't say my name. Now we get another ten minutes, right?"

I started to laugh. "Right!"

"Well, how about Saturday?" he asked. "During the day. And then the evening."

"Yeah," I said, "I'd really like that."

We talked for the rest of the ten. Then Robert said, "I can get Caroline to call back. Should I?"

"No, let's just do that only when we have to, okay?"

"Okay, see you tomorrow."

I had never lied to my parents—to my mother—before. I looked at her, messing around in the kitchen over the stove. She was frowning while she worked. *Well, she brought it on herself,* I thought. *What a dumb rule, ten minutes!*

After supper, I said, "I'm going out Saturday afternoon. And night. With Robert."

"Since when do you *tell* me what you're going to do?" Mom said.

"If I ask you'll just say no," I said, "so that's why I'm *telling.*" I thought, *we're going to have a war.*

But instead of yelling, Mom walked out of the room. I kicked really hard at a leg of the kitchen table and a dish fell off and broke.

∞

When Saturday came, I waited till we were out of the house before I asked where we were going. He wouldn't tell me in school. Not that I really cared—I had looked forward so much to being out and being with him. I tried to sound very cheerful when I said goodbye to Mom, but she just said, "Goodbye, Ronnie," which of course made me feel rotten, but I forgot it after a few minutes.

"We're going to New York," Robert said.

"The city?"

"Yup! And you know what we're going to do?"

"Window shop."

"Nope."

"Watch them skate at Rockefeller Center."

"Nope."

"How many guesses do I get?" I asked.

"One more."

"We're going to hold up Chase Manhattan Bank and be the scandal of Uniondale," I said.

"You're close," he said. "We're going to audition for a quiz show."

"I liked my guess better."

"No, I'm not kidding," he said. "We're going to audition for 'Name That Song'. They hold their contestant auditions on Saturday afternoons. I know, I wrote away and asked them."

"You're crazy," I said. "I couldn't do anything like that."

"Oh, yes you could!" he told me. "Between us, we know every song written in the twentieth century. We could get on that show. And I bet we could win something."

"You do it. I'll watch."

"All right, if you really don't want to do it," he said, "you be my moral support. Because I wouldn't try it if you weren't there."

"Okay," I told him. "That I can handle."

We took the train into the city, feeling all the time like we should hide in the john, even though we bought tickets like real people.

We got off at Penn Station and walked over to a small building on 48th Street, not far from Broadway. There was a laundry on the street floor and the auditioning place was down some outside stairs, in the basement. When we got there, a bunch of people were standing around in the cold, staring at the door.

"Are you all here for 'Name That Song'?" Robert asked no one in particular.

A lady nodded and went on staring at the door.

So we joined the people and stared at the door.

"Why are we standing here?" Robert finally asked.

"There's not enough room to wait inside," a man told us, "so we have to wait here until they're ready for the next group."

"There's a group already in there?" I asked.

"Uh huh," the man said.

When I could no longer feel any part of my feet or legs and thought for sure we'd be hospitalized for overexposure on the streets of New York, the door opened and a bunch of people walked out. The last one in the doorway was a lady with no coat on. She motioned to us.

"Wow," she said. "Get in quick before you let all the cold air in!"

Robert and I burst out laughing, which I was positive would get us eliminated right away.

We were herded down a dark hall into a room that looked just like a classroom, with desks in rows and a blackboard up front.

There weren't any kids. The lady who had brought us in looked around the room and stopped at us.

"Are you here with someone?" she asked.

Robert looked around to make sure she was talking to us, then he turned back to her. "Who, us?" he said.

"Yes. Did you just wander in, or are you here with someone?"

Robert pointed to me. "I'm here with her, she's here with me."

"I mean," the lady said slowly, "are you here with an adult?"

"No, do you have to be here with an adult?"

The lady looked exasperated. "These people are here to test for a television show called 'Name That Song'."

"Right," Robert said.

"*You're* testing for the show?"

"*He* is, I'm not," I said.

This must have totally confused her. "We've never had children test before," she said.

"Surprise!" Robert said. "You have now."

Then we went through a whole routine, where she said I'd have to leave if I wasn't auditioning, but Robert squawked about that and finally all the people in the room said, "Let 'er stay, let 'er stay," so she gave up. She had everyone fill out cards, putting their names, addresses and phone numbers on them. Then she took the people in groups of five, and played some tapes of songs. The people had to raise their hands as soon as they recognized the songs. You tried to guess the song with as few notes as possible. Robert wasn't taken until the last group, so he and I whispered the titles we knew to each other to practice. I knew Robert was going to do best. All the grownups in the different groups knew the Broadway show songs, the songs of the forties, fifties and some of the sixties, but none of them knew the rock tunes and Robert knew all of them. And sure enough, Robert had his hand up first in every category.

After everyone had a turn, the lady seemed to pick people at random for the next test. But Robert and I—and probably everyone else—knew that she was picking the people who had their hands up first the most. She picked Robert and all the people cheered.

Then she played another bunch of tapes, but there wasn't as much of each song played as before. Just the first line of the first verse of each. Robert got every one, right away, except one song called *I've Got a Loverly Bunch of Cocoanuts*, which some man not only knew, but sang for everybody. It was a funny song, and the man was pretty good. Everybody applauded, except the sour lady who was running the show.

The man who sang offered, "How 'bout the kid

sings a number?" and everyone yelled, "Yeah, yeah!" while the lady tried to calm the room down and Robert said, "No, folks, no, only when I get paid."

After that, it got tougher. Robert and three other people were left, out of the whole crowd, which I guessed to be about twenty. They stood up at the front and the lady played more tapes and less notes. Robert didn't do too well, but the other three didn't either.

"All right," the lady said, "that was fine, everyone, thank you. Now there's one more thing we have to do. We'd like to take your pictures, so we have your faces on file. We'll take them in groups of three. Now you three, just come up in front of the blackboard . . ."

She had a Polaroid camera, and as soon as the pictures came out, she cut out the faces and had the people clip them to their cards.

Finally, everyone was finished but Robert and me.

"Not you, dear," the lady said. "You didn't test."

"I want my picture taken with her," Robert insisted.

"I'm sorry, young man . . ." the lady began.

"Please?" Robert said.

Old Sourball finally melted. "Okay," she said. "Smile."

When the picture came out, she handed it to

Robert and then took another one of him alone to clip on his card.

"Thanks," Robert said to her. "That was a nice thing to do."

The lady looked at Robert's card. "Robert Rose. You did very well today. How do you know all that music, especially the old stuff? You don't look more than thirteen years old."

"Well, I *am* more than thirteen," Robert said, embarrassed, "but I know a lot of music because I've heard it all my life and I play piano."

"You're an unusual young man, Robert," the lady said.

"Thanks, I think," Robert said as we filed out behind the stragglers. Another group was waiting when we got outside. They were staring at the door.

∞

"You're an unusual young man, Robert," I said.

"I could've told you that long ago," he said. "You didn't have to get it secondhand."

He handed me the picture of us. "For your Memory Book," he said. "It's a picture of an unusual young man and his special friend."

"How, special?" I asked.

"What d'ya want it, spoon-fed?" he said.

∞

We ate an early supper at Chock Full O' Nuts on 57th Street, and then we walked back down Broadway toward Times Square. It was cold, but it was terrific.

"The people are magic," I said, believing it.

"The people are muggers, drunks and junkies," Robert said. "Walk faster."

"Are you scared?" I asked him. It never occurred to me to be scared.

"The city makes me a little nervous," he said, "especially at night. I mean, I wouldn't care if I were by myself, but . . ."

"Okay," I told him. "Let's look at the time-table and get over to the station."

The next train to Uniondale left New York at 7:30, which meant we would be home by ten after 8:00, twenty-after, tops. That was early enough so maybe Mom wouldn't be sulking. She never used to sulk. I didn't want to go home suddenly.

"What's the matter?" from Robert.

"Nothing," I said. "Why?"

"Your whole face just shifted to the left."

"Oh, I was just thinking that I wish I didn't have to go home right now."

"Yeah," Robert said. "Tell you what? After I drop you off, I'll go home and call you. Then we can prolong the day by ten minutes."

"Fun-ny!" I said. I took out the picture of us. "You know, you would've looked a lot cooler in this picture if you were smoking."

∞

I didn't ask Robert to come in, because I wasn't sure what Mom's frame of mind would be, so he left me at the door and went home.

Mom was sitting in the living room, not doing anything. I looked at that as a bad sign.

"Where were you all day?" she asked quietly.

I didn't know what to say. I never told her where I was going because I didn't know until I left the house. I had been in New York City before by myself—I had gone to meet Daddy at his office . . . plenty of times . . .

"I told you I'd be out with Robert for the day and evening," I said, avoiding it.

"Don't you think I have the right to know where my thirteen-year-old daughter is for an entire day and evening? Or did I lose that right when you started *telling* me what you were going to do?"

I definitely didn't know what to say to *that*. We'd never talked to each other like this before.

"Mom," I looked up at her. "I . . . love you."

She got up and came over to me with her arms out.

"Oh, baby, I love you, too," she said. She was crying. So was I.

The phone rang. Mom answered and then pushed it at me. "Isn't a day and evening *enough?*" she said.

"Robert?"

"Hi, there! Yours for ten big minutes!"

"No, listen, I can't talk now," I told him. "Can you call me tomorrow? Or I'll call you."

"Is she mad?" he asked.

"No, it's not that. Look, I'll talk to you tomorrow. And thanks for the day."

I hung up. "Mom?" she was out of the room. I followed her into her bedroom. "Hey, look," I began. "Off the phone in less than ten minutes. Less than five!"

"I don't feel well, Ronnie," she said, lying on her bed. "I haven't felt well in . . . a long time."

"Can I get you something?" I asked, worried.

"I never thought I'd be interfering with your life," she began, "at least not this way. You're a good kid . . . I know I've been sounding like a shrew . . . I'm sorry, but I'm not the same person I was. I don't know if I'll ever be that . . . person again." She closed her eyes. "And you're not the same."

I thought about that. No, I wasn't the same person I was when we moved here. Was I supposed to be the same?

"Mom," I said, sitting down on the bed at her feet. "Don't worry about me. I won't do anything bad. I'm just trying to keep busy, have some fun . . . Robert makes me laugh. Evelyn does, too. You should have some of that. If you stay cooped up in this house, it's just gonna get worse for you. Like Aunt Lyddie said. You should start painting again. Go see a movie, I'll go with you. Go over to Aunt Lyd's during the day. Mom?"

No answer. Her eyes were closed, so she was either asleep or ignoring me. I went into my room and counted the wallpaper.

Chapter 17

On Valentine's Day I got a stuffed giraffe from Robert. It was all red and taller than I was. He brought it over himself and said how humiliated he'd been carrying it through the streets, especially with the silly red bow around its neck. I loved it.

Arthur yelled "Pretty" at it when it came through the door.

"Hey, Arthur's really doing well!" Robert commented. "I haven't heard him say that before."

"He just started," I said. "Now he even sings 'Twinkle Twink'."

Robert laughed. "Okay, he just needs long rehearsals before he performs. What should we teach him to say next?"

"Well, I heard this man on the radio the other day, who had a talking parrot. He put the cage next to an open window and then taught the bird to scream *This is a lousy neighborhood!*"

"Fantastic!" Robert said. "Think we can teach him that?"

"The way he's been going, he can at least learn 'This is'."

"I think we should teach him the harmony line to *Love Will Keep Us Together*. Then he can join the act and you and Ev will have a two-man band."

I didn't want to talk about the act. "Watch what else he can do," I said, opening the cage door. Arthur stepped out of the cage onto my finger and then climbed across my arm and sat on my shoulder.

"Hey, that's neat," Robert said. "Will he stay there?"

"Are you kidding? I've been cleaning up after him all over the house."

"Oh, your mom must love that."

"She doesn't care. Let's put the giraffe in my room."

"Where is your mom?" Robert asked, looking around.

"Buying groceries."

"Still no sign of a let-up on the ten-minute rule?"

We sat down on my bed. "No. And we better start being more careful. I mean, having Laurie call once, okay. But you had Caroline call twice after that."

"And we talked for a whole forty minutes. Why, did you get caught?"

I shook my head. "No, but I hate to do this."

"Well," Robert said, "I don't like it either. But do we have any choice?"

Arthur flew off my shoulder and landed on Robert's picture hanging over my bed.

"He loves that picture, he always lands on it," I told Robert.

"Yeah, I can tell by those white streaks down the glass."

"Don't take it personally," I said. "Anyway, I always wipe it clean at the end of the day."

Mom came home just then and Robert left in a hurry.

∞

That night, Robert called, then had Laurie call, and then Caroline. Then, a half hour later, Evelyn called.

"Hi," she said. "I'm not calling for *my* ten minutes, I'm calling for Robert's."

"What?"

"He's here. He asked me to call, so he could talk to you. He said he's already had his own ten minutes."

"Yeah, and Laurie's and Caroline's," I told her.

"Jeez, he's grabbing the phone. Just a minute, you clod . . ."

"Ron?"

"Yes? What *now?*"

"Big Mouth's just used up four minutes. I've only got six left . . ." I started to laugh. This was so ridiculous. I was sitting there terrified of getting caught talking on the phone for more then ten minutes to the same person.

". . . And I want you to hear something. Now,

listen. Evelyn, hold the receiver near the piano. No, don't put it on the floor, dummy. Higher. Come on, Ev, higher!"

This whole time we were looking at our watches—Robert, Evelyn, me, and I was sure, my mother. Robert started to play something on the piano that I had never heard before, and I kept hearing him yell, "How much more time have I got?"

And Evelyn yelled back, "Two more minutes, play faster."

Finally, I heard someone running back to the phone. "What'd you think of that?" Robert asked.

"Beautiful!" I said. It was. "Moody blues."

"Yeah. I wrote it. You really like it?"

"You *wrote* it?"

A nasal voice, cutting in: "I yam sor-ry, your tha-ree minutes are up." Evelyn, on her upstairs extension. "Puh-lee-uz signal when ready."

"I really love it. G'bye, Evelyn." I hung up, but I couldn't stop thinking about Robert's song. And I never finished my homework.

∞

The next night I tried to do the same homework, but I couldn't concentrate on it. Robert played his song for me again that afternoon at Evelyn's and it was running through my head with about a thousand other things.

Then I got my usual trio of calls: first Robert,

then Caroline, and then Laurie, who was now asking Robert for a quarter a call and getting it. Only this time, Mom stayed by the phone, and after Laurie asked for me and I got on, Mom took the phone out of my hand and held it to her ear, listening to Robert say, "Would you believe this is costing me up to seventy-five cents a night?"

Mom just quietly hung up on him. I started to shake.

"It took a long time," Mom said, "for it to dawn on me about that trick. Every night the same thing." I didn't say anything. "Your friend is a sneak," she said. "And so are you . . ."

Chapter 18

"Ronnie?"

I rubbed my eyes. The more I rubbed them, the more they itched. Finally, I just dug my fists into them.

"*Ronnie?*"

"Huh?"

It was Miss Smith, my English teacher, and she took me by surprise because I forgot where I was.

"I'm sorry, Miss Smith," I said.

"Can you answer the question?"

I didn't know what the question was. I shook my head, thinking, *just call on someone else, please, let me alone.*

"The question was, 'Where did the story *Rip Van Winkle* first appear?' "

She hasn't called on anyone else, I thought, squinting my eyes. *She's still talking to me.* So I tried to think. But I couldn't remember who wrote *Rip Van Winkle.*

Myrna Savitch had her hand up and was waving wildly. *Oh, for God's sake,* I pleaded inside my head, *call on Myrna, call on her before she gives birth or something.*

"Myrna?" Miss Smith said. I went back to rubbing my eyes.

"It appeared in *The Sketch Book of Geoffrey Crayon, Gent.* In New York."

"Thank you, Myrn—"

"In 1819."

"Thank you, Myrna. Now, what was *The Sketch Book?* Who can tell me more about it?"

I couldn't, for sure. That morning, Mom had dropped another bomb. I couldn't see Robert any more. I could see him in groups where it couldn't be avoided, but I couldn't go out with him alone. Period.

I told Evelyn in Home Room. She couldn't believe it. But I asked her not to tell Robert until I had a chance to, first.

"I'd like to see you after class, Ronnie," I heard Miss Smith say. When the bell rang, I walked up to her desk.

"Is something wrong, Ronnie?" she asked.

"No, why?"

"Because you're usually prepared. And you look . . . rather tired."

My mind began to race. I figured that if my school work was going to suffer a little, then I ought to have a good excuse for it so the teachers wouldn't be too hard on me. I *had* a good excuse, but I couldn't tell the teacher that my mother was turning weird and wouldn't let me see my friend.

Maybe they'll think it's because of my father's death . . .

I couldn't think about my father very often. If I thought about him I would cry, and probably not be able to stop, and I didn't want to do that . . . *If he were alive and here,* I thought, *none of this stuff would be happening now at all!*

"Ronnie?" Miss Smith said.

"I'm really sorry," I began, "about not being prepared. But . . . I'm having kind of a hard time. At home, I mean. It's . . . personal." I didn't tell her I'd try harder because I wasn't sure I wanted to. My real thought, to be honest about it, was: *if she feels sorry for me, then she'll leave me alone.*

"I understand Ronnie," Miss Smith said. I wondered what she understood.

"Thank you. I have to go to Art."

∞

"What do you *mean*, we can't see each other?" Robert shrieked at me, as he dropped his books on the threshhold of the Music Room. The kids began trampling them as they walked into class.

"Get your books first," I said, miserably. "Then, I'll tell you."

He bent down to pick everything up, while the kids trampled *him*.

"What's going on anyway!" he yelled. People turned around.

"Shh! Come here." I pulled him out near the lockers.

"Last night she got a full report of Laurie's economic rip-off. From your own mouth."

"Was *that* why the phone clicked off? I thought we just got cut off and I was afraid to call back," he said.

"You should have been afraid before. She called us both 'sneaks' and said you're a bad influence on me. So that's it. I'm grounded from *you*."

"All right," he said, almost to himself. "All right, it's going to be harder, but we can get around it."

"How?" I asked.

"We'll do the 'Laurie' bit, only carry it further," he explained. "You'll just have to say you're going to Evelyn's instead of out with me. Ev'll cover for us."

"I can't do that . . . how can I do that?"

"Ron, if you don't, we won't be able to see each other," he wailed.

I knew he was right. And I knew it was wrong.

∞

Coming home that afternoon on the bus, Robert and Evelyn and I talked about the weekend. The two of them were incredible, planning and scheming like in a mystery story. If I said I was going to Evelyn's, then I wanted to really go to Evelyn's . . . Robert would just turn up there, that's all. Nothing I could do about that . . .

"Let's go down to the 'Y'," I said. "I don't think she'd object to that."

"Okay," Robert said. "We'll go to the 'Y', but we can go get pizza or something by ourselves, can't we?"

"Sure," I said. "Sure we can."

∞

"I'll drive you to the 'Y' and pick you up," Mom said.

"You don't have to do that," I told her. "I can go with Lenny, or the Racanellis, like I always do."

"Ronnie, I want to drive you. I want you to be with that boy as little as possible."

"That's totally unreasonable," I said.

"You're turning into some other person!" Mom cried.

"So are you!" I screamed back.

She ended up not driving me because she had taken a pill and was too tired, so I got to go with Lenny after all. I wanted to see Miss Fisk and Mr. Vincent. I needed to spend some time with grown-ups who made me feel happy. No matter what the vigilante committee was saying, Mr. Vincent and Miss Fisk enjoyed each other, and being with us, too.

Chapter 19

Things got worse instead of better. My school-work—the pits. All my teachers had after-class chats with me and I gave them all the same "personal problem" thing. Robert and I spent a lot of time thinking of lies to tell Mom so we could be together.

"Listen," he said, one Friday afternoon in the halls at school, "my parents are going out tomorrow night. Caroline, too. I'll be babysitting for Laurie. Come over, Ron. I guarantee Laurie'll stay out of our hair. I'll pay her a fortune!"

"I can't go to your house," I told him.

"Yes. You can. Tell your mother you're going to Evelyn's. Ev will go along with it and if your mother calls or anything, Ev will say you're in the bathroom and then call us and you can call her right back. And Ev's is close enough if you have to get over there fast."

"I hate it," I said.

"Ron, we'll have the whole house to ourselves. Peace and quiet. I'll play piano and records . . .

Look, how often do my parents go out for a whole evening?"

"Okay," I told him. "That sounds too nice to miss."

∞

"I'm going to Evelyn's Saturday night," I told Mom and remembered to add, "Okay?"

She didn't answer for a minute. Then she said, "I . . . I thought it would be nice if . . . just the two of us went out. To a movie. Like we used to."

What could I say to her? If only she had said this a couple of months ago. Finally, she was willing to go out.

"Good idea, Mom. Why don't you go with Aunt Lyd or one of your old friends or somebody like that?"

"You don't want to be with me?" she said, frowning at me.

"No, it isn't that. It's just that we're together so much—You haven't been with any grownups at all hardly. You need people your own age . . . and *I* need people *my* own age. Don't you think so?"

She didn't answer. I bet myself that I blew it. I should've said yes, I'd go with her. *Now*, I thought, *she won't go at all.*

∞

I felt crummy putting on my coat after dinner Saturday night. Especially because I knew Mom hadn't called anyone.

"Mom? I'm going."

No answer.

" 'Bye?"

Still nothing. I went into the kitchen, where she was washing dishes.

"I won't be home late." She just went on washing.

"Will you for Pete's sake say goodbye to me?"

"Goodbye," she said.

I left quickly by the front door.

I felt awful until I got to Robert's and rang the bell. The minute he answered I felt okay again. Laurie was in the living room watching TV.

"Hi, Ronnie," she said.

"Hi, Laurie."

"Come on," Robert said. "Let's go upstairs. I told Laurie she could watch TV till 11:00 if she didn't bug us. Anyway, I got a new album I want you to hear."

The album was *Teddy Wilson and His All Stars*. Robert said Teddy Wilson was a terrific jazz pianist.

"Listen, listen to that," Robert said.

"Listen to what?" I asked.

"That sound. Hear that growl? Isn't that great?"

I listened. "What is it?"

"It's a trombone. The guy's name is Vic Dickenson. Plays the most fantastic slide trombone. They call him 'the dirty old man of the trombone'."

"Robert?"

"What?"

"Have you heard anything from 'Name That Song'?"

He shook his head. "No, but they said it might be a few months. They have a whole backlog of contestants they keep on file."

"You're going to get on," I said. "I know you'll hear from them."

"Maybe," he said. "And you know what I'm going to do with the money if I win?"

"What?"

"Send my parents on a long vacation. *They* need it and *I* need it."

"You know, if you won, your father might be so proud of you that things might change for the better around here, and you could spend the money on yourself."

"Yeah. I could save for a car. Or even buy one second-hand. It'll be a little less than two years and I'll be able to get my license. Ahh, who'm I kidding? if I won any money, my father would take it and say he was entitled to it as room and board."

"He wouldn't do that!"

"Yeah, he would, Ronnie. Hey, how would you like to look through his microscope?"

"I wouldn't go near it," I said.

"No, it's fascinating. I use it all the time when he's not home. Of course, he'd kill me if he knew,

But one day, I just thought I'd take a peek to see what he was so involved in and I really got into it. Caroline showed me what to do. You know, he's got a slide with a human hair on it and it's really freaky to see what that can look like magnified! Take a look, come on."

We went into his parents' room where the microscope sat covered on a special table in the corner. Robert turned on the light and uncovered the microscope.

He went into the closet, crawled to the back, and came out with a wooden box. Then he did something with dials and a slide and said, "Okay, now look through here."

I looked. "What is it?"

"Skin. It's a piece of human skin. Can you believe it?"

"Blagh!"

"Here, look at this one," he said, quickly putting another into place and adjusting the dials again. "This is the human hair."

We looked at some more stuff, and as interesting as it was, it was making me nervous. "Robert, let's put it away," I said. "I'd really like to look at some more, but I keep thinking that, any minute, your parents will be back and they'll walk in and catch us."

"Okay," he said, "but don't worry about them walking in. They went to a war movie. My father'll probably want to sit through it twice."

"Hey," I said, "I've got an idea, let's cook something!"

"I can't cook," Robert said.

"Neither can I. Let's do it," I told him.

He started to smile. "What'll we make?"

"What do you like?"

"I like pizza, but we don't have the stuff to make it with. How about a cake?"

"Great. Let's make a cake. Do you have any recipes?" We went down into the kitchen and began to poke around. Laurie came in to see what we were doing and wanted to help.

"No," Robert told her.

"Tell you what, Laurie," I offered. "Neither of us knows what we're doing—if we need help we'll yell for you, okay?"

"Okay," she said, ". . . if I feel like it, after that brush-off." She went back to her hockey game.

We looked through a cookbook and decided to make a cheese cake. I called out the ingredients and Robert went through the cupboards and the refrigerator to see if we had everything we needed.

"Cottage cheese and cream cheese!" I yelled.

"Check."

"Eggs. Four eggs!"

"Check."

"Sugar!"

"Wait a minute . . . Check."

"Vanilla. Cornstarch."

"Check. Check."

"Flour."

"Check."

"Butter. Sour cream."

"Why didn't you say that when I was over at the refrigerator? Hold it . . . Butter, sour cream. Right."

"Lemon juice."

"Lemon juice? You mean lemons we have to squeeze?"

"I guess so, it says lemon juice."

Both of us looked at each other and then together we yelled out, *"Laurie!"*

She appeared.

"Do we have any lemons?" Robert asked.

"No."

"Well, what do we do about lemon juice? Is there something else you can use instead?"

"Oh," she said. "Lemon juice is different. You don't need lemons."

"What do you mean?" Robert asked.

Laurie held out her hand. "It'll cost ya," she said.

Robert shook his head. "Laurie, that's rotten!" he said.

She shrugged and started back into the living room. "Okay," she said. "Get your cooking lessons from Julia Child."

"Wait a minute, Laurie," I said. "Come on. What do we use?"

"All right, Ronnie, this'll be a freebie 'cause I

like you." She stuck out her tongue at her brother. "Lemon juice comes in a bottle. Didn't you really know that?"

"Uh uh," I said.

"Well, it does," she said, reaching into the refrigerator. "We have a little bottle of it way in the back here . . ." She pulled it out. "Here. But anything after this . . . you pay!"

"She has a gene for money-grubbing," Robert said. "That pretty little ten-year-old with that soft, blonde hair and those adorable dimples will be a millionaire-executive before she's twenty-one. And probably most of her money will be mine!" He smiled. He and Laurie liked each other a lot, I knew. But they also teased each other like crazy, with Laurie coming out on top most of the time.

"Laurie is my father's favorite," Robert had said once.

"How do you know?" I asked him.

"Because if Laurie does something really aggravating, irritating and scream-worthy, my father will yell at *me* . . . or worse."

"Really?"

"Yeah. I don't know why Caroline hasn't gotten her own place yet, now that she's working. But I guess she's kind of out of firing range now. And she does pay them something every week."

I couldn't stand to think of Robert in any kind of pain. I honestly couldn't.

"It says you have to strain the cottage cheese and the cream cheese through a sieve," I said.

"How do you do that?"

"Where's your sieve?" I asked him.

He looked at me, I looked at him, and once again, both of us yelled together: *"Laurie!"* and burst out laughing.

She came in, open hand first. Robert was just about to put the unwrapped cream cheese into it when the phone rang. Both of us turned white. Robert picked up the receiver.

"H'lo?"

Pause.

"Okay, thanks," He hung up and turned to me. "That was Ev. Call your mother. Ev told her you were in the bathroom . . ."

I felt dizzy and sat down. "All right. Just give me a minute . . ."

"Take a deep breath," Laurie offered.

I took a few and then called.

"It wasn't anything important," Mom said. "I . . . I just felt badly about the way you left the house and . . . thought I'd tell you so. That's all."

I should have felt better but I felt worse. "Thanks, Mom," I said. "Thanks for calling."

I felt Robert's hand on my shoulder as I hung up.

"I think I ought to go over to Evelyn's," I said.

"Why?" from Laurie.

"Because she thinks I'm there. What if she calls again? Evelyn can't say I'm in the bathroom again, she'll plug me up with Kaopectate!"

"She won't call again," Robert said. "She won't. Come on, Ronnie . . . don't leave."

"Oh, damn," I said. *Everything is getting spoiled*, I thought. "Listen, why don't we take this stuff over to Evelyn's and cook there?"

"That's no fun," Robert said. "Evelyn knows *how* to cook. Takes all the joy out of it."

"But I don't know what my mother's going to do!" I told him. "I can't have a good time if I'm worrying about getting caught every minute."

"All right, all right," he said, "we'll go over there."

"You can't," Laurie said. "You're babysitting, remember?"

"Aw, Laurie . . ." Robert said.

"I don't wanna be in the house alone. I don't, Robert, otherwise I'd let you go," Laurie said.

"Come with us," Robert said.

"I'm in my pajamas!"

"Who cares? Put on your coat and come with us."

"Robert, if they come back early and we're not here, do you know what could happen?"

Robert suddenly put his hand up to his mouth and took a breath. "Oh, my God!"

"What?" I asked.

"The slides! I forgot to put the slides back in the closet! Someone up there must really love me to make me remember in time!" He raced upstairs and I went into the hall for my coat.

"Robert?" I yelled from the front door. "I'm going over to Evelyn's for a little while and then home. I'm sorry. I can't stand this!"

"Wait!" he yelled from upstairs. "Wait just a minute! I'll think of someth—"

Crash.

Tinkle, tinkle . . . tinkle.

Clink.

Laurie's face turned chartreuse. Mine must have, too. Neither of us moved. Then both of us knocked into each other racing up the stairs. Robert was sitting on the floor in the upstairs hall, and all around him were bits of broken glass . . . and a wooden box.

Nobody said anything. Then Laurie started to cry. "He'll kill you, Robert. You know he will . . ."

"It's okay, Laurie, it's okay," Robert said. He was very calm and very pale. "Don't cry. I know what I'll do."

"What?"

"I'll clean up all this stuff. Then I'll put whatever isn't broken back in the box . . ." We all looked around, but it didn't look like there were too many unbroken slides left.

". . . And then I'll just put the box back in the closet like nothing happened. He won't know anything until the next time he opens the box and finds them missing. And then we'll all just deny knowing anything about it. That's all."

"He won't believe us," Laurie said, still crying.

"He won't be able to prove it," Robert said. He was talking very quietly. He sounded like he was a-hundred-and-eight years old.

Laurie just sobbed louder. "He doesn't *have* to prove it!" she cried. "What has proof got to do with anything!"

"We'll just deny it, Laurie, that's it. We can handle it."

While they were talking, I was picking up bits of glass. I went into Robert's room and got his waste-basket, dumped out his dirty socks and began putting the glass in. I still had my coat on.

Robert bent down to help. "Laur, go get the vacuum cleaner. Stop crying and go get it!"

When we were finished there wasn't a trace of glass. Robert and his sister decided to clean up the kitchen and go to bed. I decided to go straight home.

∞

The lights were on when I came into the house. I hollered for Mom but no one answered. I started to panic and run through the house. She was nowhere around. Before I could figure out what to do, I heard the front door open and I ran toward it. Mom's hand was on the doorknob and she was staring at me.

"Where'd you go?" I asked, trying to sound cheerful. "I didn't see a note . . ."

She went on staring at me.

"You didn't have to come back early because of me," I said.

"I went to Evelyn's to pick you up. It was getting late . . . I didn't want you to walk. Besides, I wanted us to talk."

I thought, *I can't stand any more.*

"Her brother answered the door. He said you weren't there. He said you weren't there all night."

I don't care, I thought. *I don't even care.*

"You're a sneak *and* a liar," she said. And she went to bed.

∞

I didn't think things could get much worse. I was grounded from everything outside of school, including phone calls. From anybody. Mom and I didn't even talk to each other.

At school, Robert was a wreck waiting for his father to discover the almost-empty slide box. We were so unhappy we didn't even get in trouble in Social Studies. Mr. Vincent commented about it. And he asked us after class once, why he hadn't seen either of us at the "Y" lately. We didn't know what to say.

"If you don't cheer up a little, I'm gonna burst into tears," Evelyn said at the end of the week.

"I wish you would," Robert said. "Your happiness is making me miserable."

"That's more like it, buddy," she said. "Come on, let's have a little sarcasm. What can I *do* to make you guys laugh a little?"

"Whatever it is, it'll have to be during school," I told her. "After that, I have Chair Privileges only."

"What're Chair Privileges?"

"I can go anywhere I want, as long as I don't get up off the living room chair," I answered.

"That bad?"

I nodded. "All we do at home is sit around and glare at each other."

"I wish that's all that would happen to me," Robert said, "when my father discovers those missing slides . . . And today he'll have more time than usual to discover them."

"Why?" I asked.

"He had to drive out to Huntington early this morning on business. Which means he'll probably be home by 2:30 or 3:00 this afternoon. Which means he'll have more time for his hobby. Which means . . ."

"He'll head straight for his microscope," Evelyn finished.

"And that's just when you get home from school," I said.

"Ohh, no," he said. "Not today, I'm putting it off as long as possible. Even Laurie's made plans for this afternoon."

"Have you told Caroline or your mother?" Evelyn asked.

"No one. That would get them involved, too." He walked away toward his next class. Evelyn and I walked out to lunch.

"He's going to be late," I said.

"I've never seen him like that before," Evelyn said. "He's *so* down. I mean, his father's a beast, but I think what's getting to him is all this *waiting*. I mean, it's been . . . what? . . . five days? Six? And old Harlan hasn't hit the closet once. God."

I had an idea.

I suddenly knew how I could help Robert.

∞

Mom wasn't home after school, thank God, otherwise I'd have had to use the pay phone in the drug store on the corner.

I was so terrified, I was shaking, but I knew I had to do it and I knew I didn't have much time, so there really wasn't room for chickening out.

I dialed Robert's number.

"Hello?"

"Caroline? This is Ronnie. Ronnie Rachman."

"Hi, Ronnie. Robert isn't here."

"I know. I want to talk to . . . your father."

"Who?"

"Your father. Is he home?"

"I'm sorry, Ronnie, did you say you want to talk to my *father?*"

"Yes."

"Okay. Just a minute."

"Hello?"

I heard that voice and lost my own. I thought, *it's not too late, hang up, hang up right now!*

"Mr. Rose?"

"Yes? What is it?"

"Mr. Rose, this is Ronnie Rachman."

"Yes?"

Oh, God. "Mr. Rose I was at your house last weekend and while everybody was downstairs I found your microscope and slides when I walked into your room by mistake thinking it was Caroline's and I just had to look at it. I just had to and by mistake I dropped your slide box and a lot of the slides broke and I just couldn't stand it any more and I had to tell you."

There.

Done.

There was a long pause before:

"You what?" And then the phone went dead in my hand. I supposed he had gone to check the box to see if what I said was true. I thought, *okay, go check the box, and then after about two minutes, the phone will ring.*

Ten minutes went by. No ring. Half an hour.

Mom walked in the door. I walked into my room.

I spent hours counting my wallpaper and waiting for the phone to ring. I kept thinking, *I did a good thing: I took the waiting away from Robert, and now I have it.*

Chapter 20

I couldn't use the phone and no one could call me.
I couldn't find out what was happening. I thought,
*Robert must be home by now. And he's found out what I
did. What will he do?*

I don't know when I got off my bed onto my
knees—something I'd done only two times before
in my life: once to ask for a two-wheeled bike for
my ninth birthday and once the same year, when I
asked for Daddy's arm not to be broken after he fell
while helping me learn to ride the two-wheeled
bike. I did get both things.

Now I asked for Robert to go along with what
I'd done; to please not think he was a hero and tell
his father he'd done it. I closed my eyes tight and
prayed and prayed until my mother knocked on
my door to say dinner was ready.

Another talkless meal. I sat down opposite her at
the kitchen table. Terrific. Hamburger Helper.
Anyway, it didn't matter what it was, there was no
way I could eat.

"I was with Aunt Lydia this afternoon . . ."
Mom said.

"Uh huh."

"She wants us to come and spend the weekend with her and Uncle Fred."

I hope we go, I thought. *Oh, I hope we go. Can we leave right now?*

"What did you tell her?" I asked.

"I said we would."

"Okay," I said.

And then the phone rang.

"*I'll* get it," Mom said. Naturally. If she were in the middle of a shower, covered with soap, she'd yell "*I'll* get it!" With this phone call, though, it didn't make any difference. I stared at a plate full of Hamburger Helper and listened.

"Wait a second, talk a little slower . . . She what? . . . Please, I still can't understand . . . She broke what? . . . Your *what?* Well, how did she . . . Yes, but . . . Well, how much did they . . . Yes, I certainly will . . . But I don't . . ."

And then she was staring at a dead receiver, just as I had before.

"That was Robert's father."

I nodded.

"You know what he said?"

Nod.

"He said his whole family spent the afternoon restraining him from coming over here and 'breaking your little arm'."

I licked my lips.

"Was that when you were at Robert's on Saturday night?"

"Yes."

"Or have you been sneaking over there since?"

"NO!"

She stopped speaking for a minute. Then, "He
said that you're going to have to pay for every last
one of them."

"Did he say how much?"

"He said it was hard to put a price tag on them.
Finally he said fifty dollars. Someone in the background kept yelling, 'twenty-five!' "

"Robert?"

"No. It must have been his wife. Anyway, he
settled for thirty." She sat back down, put both her
arms on the table and looked at me. "Just what are
you turning into, anyway?"

I didn't answer. I was wondering what Robert
had thought, what he'd done.

"Ronnie, *answer me!*"

"What? I didn't hear you."

"I said, how are you going to get the money? To
pay Mr. Rose?"

"I don't know. But I'll get it."

Mom made her lips very thin. "Darn right, you
will," she said, and got up to clear the table.

∞

I figured we'd leave for Aunt Lyddie's early the
next morning, since neither of us wanted to be

alone with each other a whole lot. But what happened was, I kept waking up all night and having these weird dreams, so that by the time the morning came, I was so exhausted I didn't get out of bed until 10:30.

One of my dreams was of being at Coney Island, and in the beginning it was terrific. I was with Robert, and we went on all the really tough rides, and ate a lot of junk and had a super time. Then we decided to go on those electric cars, the ones that have room for only one person, the driver, and you just steer the thing around and bump into all the other cars on the floor. And that's it, you just keep on knocking into everybody else, they knock you from behind, spin you around . . .

I've always liked that ride, but in this dream, I got into one car and Robert got into another one . . . and then I couldn't find him. But my mother was in still another car and I saw her coming right for me. I tried to ram her first but I couldn't move, there was something wrong with the steering wheel. And while I was trying to figure out what was wrong, I saw Mr. Rose in another car and he was heading right for me, too. And then, everybody on the floor saw that I was trapped with no steering and they all thought I was the one to get, so they all headed for me. I just put both my arms up over my face and screamed and then I woke up.

I think I might have been screaming in real life,

too, because I could have sworn I heard my own voice while I was thrashing around. But Mom didn't come in and with dreams you never can be sure anyway.

∞

That Saturday was easy once we got to Lynbrook. Aunt Lyd and Uncle Fred went crazy trying to make us feel at home and comfortable and we could talk to them, not to each other. I carried it off okay, but Mom never got out of 'park'.

My cousins, Eddie and Rick, weren't home. They're both in college, but they had a lot of records and things in their room for me to play with, so after one of Aunt Lyd's typical lunches of mushy stuff in bowls covered with Saran Wrap, which you were supposed to spread on bread, I escaped in there, closed the door and worried about Robert.

After about an hour, Aunt Lydia knocked on the door. I didn't say anything, so she just came in. I looked up at her from the floor, where I was listening to Peter Frampton with my cousin's headphones.

"Can I talk to you, Ronnie?"

I chewed on my upper lip. I had to think that over. If Aunt Lyd could help, then I'd be glad to talk. But if she was just going to be another Mom, I wanted no part of it.

While I was thinking it over, she sat down on a

desk chair next to me, so I could tell what I answered didn't matter.

"I just had a long talk with your mother . . . She's very unhappy about you, Ronnie."

So far, it was easy. I hadn't said a word.

"She said your whole personality was changing, and she's terribly worried. Of course, honey, it's expected that you'd go through a bad time . . . We all are."

She was talking about Daddy. That's what the teachers thought it was all about. I still didn't even want to think about Daddy. It was getting harder and harder to picture his face, which drove me crazy.

"Ronnie, talk to me. I want you to tell me what it is."

All right, I thought. *You asked for it.*

"You think I'm changing? What about *her?*"

"Your mother?"

"Out of nowhere, from nothing, come these *rules*. Only ten minutes for each phone call; no seeing my . . . friend, except in groups, not alone; then, no seeing him at all. Or anyone else!"

"But," Aunt Lydia said, "in all fairness, didn't you sneak around behind your mother's back? And break the rules, so that she had to make stricter ones?"

"I had to. The rules weren't fair to begin with. I never used to have any rules like that."

"Honey, you have to realize what your mother is feeling. She loved your Daddy very, very much, and now she feels completely alone. Try to understand: right now, you're all she has."

I sat up and put the phones in my lap. "But that's not fair," I said. "I shouldn't be all she has. She's not all *I* have. I love her, but I'm getting claustrophobia."

Aunt Lydia sighed. "You're right . . . to feel the way you do. But you can't judge every situation that comes up by 'right' and 'wrong'. Your mom does need something outside herself and outside you, but what she's feeling now is normal, Ronnic, and everything takes time."

"Yeah."

"Listen, Ronnic," she said more sternly. "This is a very lonely time for your mother. Do you know what it's like for her to walk into an empty bedroom every night? And get into an empty bed by herself? When for all those years, she spent the nights with the man she loved, who loved her?"

"I know . . . it's hard for her, I know that."

"It's a different kind of loneliness," Aunt Lydia went on. "You're old enough now to begin to think about someone beside yourself. *Really* think. Make some allowances."

"Well, I can't make all of them."

"No. You can't. But you can put a few grownup ideas in your head. Your mother is an independent woman, she always has been, but even independent people need more than themselves. She needed your father to *share* with—to share the responsibilities, the problems, the *joys*. To share love with. You've lost a father. That's a terrible thing. But your mother has lost a partner—a full partner in her life."

I looked down at my shoes.

"These are things you shouldn't have to deal with at this time in your life," Aunt Lydia said quietly. "But sometimes you don't have any choice."

∞

In the car going home on Sunday, I said, "I had a long talk with Aunt Lyd."

"I did, too," Mom said.

"I'm sorry if I've been selfish," I told her.

"I think we'll both have to try harder with each other," she said.

I wanted to ask her if that meant my punishment was over, but I didn't. I looked out the window. We were driving down Pacific Avenue, turning left on Cornwell. I hadn't been along this route since Robert and I had hitched home from the Lynbrook Station about a hundred years ago. What a different ride that had been . . . Such a good time . . . Oh, Robert . . .

Robert. All weekend I had made up stories in my head about things that might happen: what I would do if he told; how I would get the money if he didn't; and what I was going to say to him, because he would surely blow his top at what I did.

But I had no way to get any answers until school the next day. Another night without sleep.

Chapter 21

I hoped just that one morning he might be on the bus, but he wasn't. Anyway, I knew he had Band first period on Mondays, so I got excused from French to go to the bathroom and rushed down to the Music Room.

I looked through the glass door. Someone else was playing the piano and Robert was sitting on the side watching. I knocked on the door and told the girl who answered it that I had a message for Robert Rose and could he please come out in the hall for a minute. Then I watched while she tapped him. He looked up, saw me, jumped a mile out of his seat, and rushed for the door, ramming his side into the corner of someone's desk. I winced.

He closed the door behind him and grabbed for my arm, yanking me out of the vision of the kids in the room.

"What in the name of—Why did you do that!" If you can yell while you're whispering, that's what he did.

"To take the heat off ya, sweetheart," I said, imitating Humphrey Bogart, but he ignored it.

"My God, I couldn't believe it when I got home Friday. I tried and tried to call you all Saturday, and Sunday. I know I probably wouldn't have gotten through, but . . ."

"We were in Lynbrook. At my aunt's."

". . . but I couldn't stand it!"

"Did you tell him?"

He sighed and relaxed. "No. I started to . . . I wanted to . . . But you should have seen him, Ron, he was absolutely purple. The best thing for everybody was that the person he thought did it wasn't available. To be ripped into shreds. The only fallout I got was to be smacked on the side of the head for having you for a friend."

"I figured that. There wasn't anything he could really do to *me*."

"I figured that, too, but I felt like such a dumb coward . . ."

"Don't be a nut," I told him.

He put both his hands on my shoulders. "Nobody's ever . . ." He stopped and shook his head.

"What are friends for?" I said, smiling.

"*I'm* going to get the money, though," he said. "Don't worry at all about that."

"How?"

"I'll think of something," he said. "I could mow lawns."

"In March?"

"Well . . . I could play piano somewhere. I don't know. But don't you worry about it."

"No good," I said.

"Why?"

"Because my mother thinks I owe your father. And she said I have to earn it myself."

The door to the Music Room opened and the teacher poked his head out.

"What's going on out here? Robert? What are you doing in the hall?"

"Uh . . . Sorry. I had a message . . . a call from home. She—uh—she brought it from the office," Robert said, and turned to me. "Thanks, uh, very much. I'll handle it . . . it's okay," and he disappeared back into his class.

I spent the rest of the school day trying to think of ways to earn thirty dollars, and figured the only way was babysitting. I had done a little in Lynbrook, but none here since we moved. I didn't even know anybody with young kids. The only time we saw any neighbors was the first week we moved, when two couples dropped in to say welcome, but they didn't have any children.

By the time Gym came, eighth period, I felt too tired to even get through the calisthenics. Miss Fisk made the girls do relays and called me over.

"I'm worried about you, kiddo," she said.

"You and the world," I told her.

"Well?"

Why was she the only one who always made me feel like crying?

I looked at my sneakers. "I . . . don't know."

"I've been looking for you down at the 'Y'," she said. "I think you need to get out of yourself more. You haven't been going out much, have you?"

Now, that was a laugh. But I was a straight man. "No," I said. "I haven't."

"Hmmm," she said, and thought a minute. Then she said, "Feel like playing any more?"

"Not really."

"Okay, go get dressed."

∞

"I thought about babysitting," I told Robert and Evelyn on the way home. "Do you know anyone who uses babysitters? A lot?"

Robert looked angry. "I told you, forget about it. I'm going to get the money."

I thought, *but where? And what difference will it make who gets the money, anyway, as long as we get it? It will be easier for me.* But I didn't want to hurt his feelings . . .

"No, look," I said, "if I babysit, not only do I show my mother I'm working, but I also get out of the house!"

"Yeah!" Robert said, his face lighting up. "Then we get to see each other. We can *both* babysit!"

". . . Only we'll have to be pretty darn careful," I said.

"Poor children," Evelyn said.

"Well, start lining up some parents. Easter Vacation's coming and the kids'll be out of school. The parents will be glad to get out for a couple of evenings," I said.

"I never babysat," Evelyn said. "Too boring—"

"I know," Robert interrupted. "I'll ask Caroline. Maybe there's a family she knows through the hospital. Someone with a sick child to be read to or minded during the day or something."

"Terrific. Ask her. I'll work the whole vacation if I can," I told him.

∞

"You have a teacher who cares a lot about you," Mom said, when I walked in.

I thought, *what now?*

"A very nice person, by the name of Jane Fisk. She just called, not ten minutes ago."

"She's my Gym teacher. And she's at the 'Y'. I told you about her . . ."

"Oh. Yes. She came to . . . the funeral, didn't she?" Mom asked quietly. "Well, she called to tell me she thought you were crawling into a shell."

I had to smile. "Not getting out enough?"

Mom smiled. "That's what she said. And . . . Lydia said I . . . ought to back off from you a little, too. So I've decided . . . to allow you to see your friends, and go down to the 'Y'—"

I started to jump up and down like a little kid.

"*But* . . ."

Down.

"I don't want you seeing Robert Rose. I don't like his actions, I don't like him encouraging you to disobey me, and I want you to stay away from him."

"But . . ."

"I understand he will be in the group of friends you like to be with, but not alone, Ronnie. Not . . . alone."

I decided not to get upset. One step at a time, I said to myself, take it one step at a time.

"Well, look," I told her, "I think that the best way for me to earn the money to pay Mr. Rose for the slides is by babysitting. And since I don't know anyone with little kids, Robert said in school that he would ask Caroline if she knew anyone at the hospital who might need someone. So he might call about that, and can I talk?"

"Caroline can give you the information," she said.

Still the dumb games.

"Oh, all right," she said and walked away as I sank into the couch.

∞

My first babysitting job didn't come through Caroline. It came through Evelyn's brother Lenny, whose date couldn't go with him to a country music concert, unless she could find a sitter for her little sister. So, naturally, Lenny asked Evelyn, who asked me. The name was Singer and they lived on one of the President streets. Coolidge. Mr. Singer was supposed to pick me up at 7:00 and bring me home around midnight.

Robert said, "I'll be there at 8:00, to give everybody enough time."

"No," I said. "We're going to play it safe. We'll talk on the phone, but don't come over. Please, Robert. Next time, maybe."

"No visitors," Mom said. "I hope that's understood. Not only because of our personal problem, but because people don't like their babysitters to entertain friends."

"Our" personal problem, I thought. "No visitors," I said.

"And don't stay on the phone. The Singers may try to call you to check on their little girl."

"Don't stay on the phone," I said.

∞

The little girl's name was Lois. She was six and nasty. She was allowed to stay up until 8:00, so I had about an hour to entertain her after the Singers left.

"*Read* to me," Lois demanded.

"What do you want me to read?"

"This!"

"Lois, that's *People* magazine."

"I know. Read it."

"Lois, it's a grownup magazine," I told her.

"I know it, stupid! It has a picture of Elton John in it. Read me about him."

I wanted to sock her.

"Listen, I don't think your parents would like me to read about Elton John to you. Why don't you get a story book or something?"

"I hate story books. Read me about Elton John."

"How about if I *tell* you a story?" I said.

"About what?" she said, with her lower lip stuck out.

"About a nasty little girl, who got so fresh, her babysitter sent her to bed an hour early."

"You can't do that," Lois sneered.

"Oh, yes I can," I said. "And I'm just about to."

"I'll tell my mommy. And she won't let you babysit any more for me. And she'll tell all her friends and they won't let you babysit any more, either. And then you won't have any job and you'll have to stay home all by yourself."

"Damn it, Lois . . ."

"Huhhhh! You said 'damn'," she squeaked.

"Doesn't anyone ever say that to you?" I said, clenching my teeth.

"Daddy does and Mommy always yells at him. Read!"

"Okay, okay." I picked up the magazine. " 'Last month, on a television special, Elton John . . .

"Lois, I'm not reading this to you. Look, how about a snack?" I suggested.

"Only if I can fix it."

I wanted to push her face in. "Fine. I'll go with you."

"No! You have to stay here."

"All right, all right, I'll stay here."

Next time, I mumbled to myself, I only work with babies. Nobody over two.

I sat down to read the article about Elton John.

About ten minutes later, Lois appeared with her snack. I screamed when I saw her face.

"What's wrong?" she said calmly.

"What's that all over your face? It looks like blood!"

"It's strawberry jam," she said.

I looked at her plate. It was smeared with jam and, I guessed, peanut butter. So were her pajamas, robe, bare feet and braids.

"What did you do?" I asked, feeling weak.

"Made a sandwich," she said, stuffing the goo in her mouth with her fingers.

"Where's the bread?" I demanded. "There's no bread."

"I hate bread," she said and plopped her jam-covered self down on the white furry couch.

I went into the kitchen. Disaster. They could've filmed it for the Six O'Clock News. It took me until 8:00, her bedtime, to mop up. I figured I'd worry about the couch after she was asleep.

"Okay, Lois, we have to get you cleaned up," I told her.

"Not," she said.

"What?"

"I said '*not*'*!* I hate to clean up."

"You can't go to bed wearing jam."

"Can too."

The phone rang. Lois and I raced for it but I won, getting my jeans covered with jam in the process.

"Hi. How's it going?" It was Robert.

"I can't talk to you now," I told him, "I've got a kid here you wouldn't believe. I thought they only made kids like this for TV."

"Why?" he asked.

"I'll have to call you back," I said, "but I'll tell you this: Our parents should thank their lucky stars they got *us* and not *this!*" I hung up.

Lois was licking the jam off her braids when I turned around. I finally decided I didn't care what she told her mommy and daddy, it was time for brute force. I marched her upstairs, screaming her sticky little head off, and sponged her down. She wouldn't tell me where her pajamas were kept, so I had to go through all her drawers before I found them. I plunked her, sobbing, into bed and went downstairs to put her dirty stuff into the washing machine.

Then I called Robert.

"This kid is a monster," I said. "How many did we say we wanted?"

"Twelve," he answered.

"Well, cut that down."

"To how many?"

"Minus twelve," I answered, "and counting."

"You mean no Joey, Chloe, or Zoe?"

"And no Doris, Morris and Cloris, either."

"I'm crushed," Robert sobbed.

"Let's have puppies," I told him. "Listen, I can't stay on too long. They may be calling to find out how their kid is. I'm deciding whether or not to tell them."

"Okay," he said, "but if they do call, get back to me afterward, because they probably won't phone again."

I told him I would and hung up. The Singers never called and I was asleep on the couch when they came home.

My eyes were still closed when I heard Mrs. Singer say, "What's that smell?"

"Lysol," I mumbled.

"Did you say 'Lysol'?"

I sat up, pushing my hair out of my eyes. "Lois got jam on the couch. I had to clean it up with Lysol."

"Why did you let her eat *jam* on this *couch!*" Mrs. Singer cried.

With those words, I thought, *my babysitting future is sealed.*

∞

I was wrong. I got a call the following week from someone who got my name from someone else.

Beverly said that all you have to do is put the word out that you're available for babysitting and the calls come rolling in.

"How about this time?" Robert wanted to know. "Can I come over?"

"Let me check it out first," I told him. "I'll call you when I get there."

The house was on Chestnut, Robert's block. He knew the people, at least his mother did, and if they saw him there or heard he was there it wouldn't be too bad. He could say that he was just bringing over some homework or something for me.

Mom hadn't checked up on me at the last job— she hadn't even called. So, I figured, maybe it would be safe to try.

This time there were two kids, two and four years old. Both of them were in bed and asleep when the father brought me over there at 8:30. Their last name was Kelsey.

They had bean bag chairs and a color TV with a big round screen and lots of neat magazines. *This, I thought, is what babysitting ought to be like. Where you don't even see the kids.*

I gave it an hour and then called Robert.

"All's quiet on the Western front," I told him. "You can cross, but keep your head down."

"I'll knock three times," he said. "What's the password?"

" 'I've Got a Loverly Bunch of Cocoanuts'," I said.

He was there in two seconds flat, with two bags of popcorn and a six-pack of 7-Up.

The phone rang only once and it was just the Kelseys, asking about Kenny and Frances. I almost said "Who?", when I realized they meant the kids. I'd forgotten they were there. Out of guilt, I went to check on them and they were still breathing and everything.

Robert and I watched "Westworld," this movie about the future, where you can arrange a vacation of your own fantasy, anything you want, and the owners of the resort have these robots who look just like people and help you act your fantasy out. It works great until something goes wrong with the robots and they start killing the guests.

Then Robert and I played "Westworld."

After that we watched Carol Burnett, and then we *did* Carol Burnett. Robert was Tim Conway and I was Carol, and then *I* was Tim and *he* was Carol.

We were about to watch the news and then *do* the news, when he spotted two headlights pulling into the Kelsey's driveway. It had to be Mom! It was too early for the Kelseys.

Everything in my stomach started churning.

"I'll run upstairs into the kids' room!" Robert said, quickly grabbing his coat and a bag of popcorn.

"No, no, not the kids' room! She may go in there. Get in an upstairs closet! Hurry, hurry!"

He disappeared up the stairs, but was back down instantly.

"Get up there!" I yelled frantically. I was running around doing absolutely nothing.

"My hat, hand me my ski hat!" There was panic in his voice. "Quick, it's on the couch!"

I grabbed the hat and threw it up the stairs where he caught it on the run.

I searched the room wildly for any traces that showed two people had been there, but couldn't find anything. 7-Up cans, yeah, but I could've had them all.

I was ready to face the knock on the front door, hoping I could speak in a normal voice, when a man's voice called my name from behind. Naturally, I screamed.

"Ronnie, hey, it's only me!" It was Mr. Kelsey, followed by his wife.

"We came through the basement, because we put the car in the garage. I'm awfully sorry we scared you," Mrs. Kelsey said.

"I . . . I . . . You're early," I said.

"Oh, I know," she said flopping on a bean bag chair. "It was a terrible party. Dull food, dull people . . ."

Robert! What if he thinks it's Mom and doesn't realize the owners came home. If he had been there with me in the living room, we could have handled them like we planned. But there was no way I could explain him in the closet.

"Get your coat, Ronnie, I'll take you home," Mr. Kelsey said, yawning.

Oh, my God.

"Listen, before I go, let me just go up and check on the kids for you," I said.

"*I'll* do that, honey," Mrs. Kelsey said.

"No, no. Let me. I—I like to finish my job before I go. You just stay—right—there!" I bolted for the stairs.

I whispered "Robert!" as quietly as I could but got no answer, which meant he couldn't know what was happening down there, so I started softly tapping on closed doors that looked like closets. One of them tapped back.

"Look, I can't talk," I said. "It's the Kelseys, they're home. They're going to take *me* home. What can we do?"

"I'll stay in here until they go to bed. Then I'll sneak out the front door. Don't worry, just get out of here."

"Don't worry!"

"Shh! No, just go, just go," he insisted.

"All right," I told him, "but do me this one favor. When you get out of here and get home, call my house. Just let the phone ring once and hang up. That way I'll know everything is okay. If you get caught, let it ring twice."

"What good will *that* do? Then you won't know what happened. You'll worry all night."

"Ronnie?" from downstairs.

"Do it, just do it," I whispered and went down.

∞

That night I got my first headache. I mean, my first really bad one. It started in Mr. Kelsey's car and by the time I got home, I could hardly even see. I went straight to my room, wrapped my pillow around my head, and started rocking back and forth. But it didn't help. The pain was so bad, I didn't even think about poor Robert, doubled up under a bunch of bath towels in someone's linen closet. Luckily, Mom was too tired to notice that I hadn't said much when I got in, and she went straight to bed.

At quarter to 1:00, the phone rang. I unwrapped my head and sat up. Once. *Only once, please! Once. Thank you. Ohh, thank you.*

The pain in my head began to pull away. That's the only way to put it—pull away. It wasn't gone, but it wasn't there, if that makes any sense. I had a feeling that if I just lay very still and didn't move, the pain would forget about me. But if I moved, it would say, Aha! *There* you are!, and zonk me again. So there was like a big empty space in my head where the pain was, and might be again. I crawled into the empty space and fell asleep.

Chapter 22

The headache that night was what Evelyn would call "the opening number." It was followed by a whole bunch of them, and it didn't take much to bring one on. Since I got my period right after the first one, I thought it might have had something to do with that, but I'd had my period for a whole year before and never got headaches with it. I guess I really knew it had nothing to do with that.

Of course, I didn't mention the headaches to Mom. She had enough problems. So if I felt one coming on, I just went into my room. They were bad, they were really bad ones.

One came on after I was supposed to be at the "Y" after school, helping to paint the big recreation room. I brought old clothes to school so Mom would think I was really going, but then Robert and I went off by ourselves to the record shop. The record shop was right next door to Abelard's, this sportswear store, and who was walking out of it just as we passed by, but Aunt Ruth. She gave me a big hello and I just acted like nothing was wrong, but the whole time I kept wondering if she would mention to Mom that she saw me. There was just this little ache behind my left eye for the rest of the afternoon, but by the time I walked into my house it was a full-blown hurricane. That's when I got the idea of giving my headaches names, like they do with real hurricanes. That way I could see how frequently they came. Alphabetical order: girl, boy—girl, boy. I didn't remember if I had had three or four so far, so I decided to start all over again with "A." This one would be "Abigail."

Headache Frederick came during school, around mid-April. That was the worst. I could handle it at home, where I could just close my eyes and rock back and forth with a pillow wrapped around my head, but in school, it was not only painful, it was embarrassing. Of all times it happened during Social Studies, seventh period, with Mr. Vincent. And Robert in the class. I waited so long before I did anything about it that I started crying at my desk, and Mr. Vincent had to stop everything and take me to the nurse. Walking from my seat to the classroom door with Mr. Vincent's arm around me was the longest walk I ever took in my life.

"Do you get headaches like these frequently, Ronnie?" the nurse asked me.

"No. Yes."

"Beg pardon?" the nurse said.

I had to think. If I said no, which was my first impulse, then she might call my mother about it because then headaches were unusual for me. But if I said yes, then she would figure my mother knew about it all along and she might not call. The pain started to get worse. When I was a little kid, if my parents said not to do something and I did it anyway, I always told them about it, even if I didn't get caught. I hated to lie, I *never* lied. *Now,* I thought, *I'm becoming so good at it I can't even tell what is the truth any more.*

I told the nurse it was a sinus headache and I got them all the time. And I told her my mother worked and couldn't get to school.

I lay down on the cot, put my arms around my head and rocked and cried. Till it got better.

I missed Gym and Math. Robert and Evelyn were standing outside the nurse's door when I finally felt well enough to sit up and look around. Their faces were white.

They both spoke at once: "Ronnie, what . . . ?" "Ronnie, how do you . . . ?"

I smiled. "I'm okay, Doctor Welby. The operation was a success."

"How come your mother didn't come and get you?" Evelyn wanted to know.

"I wouldn't let the nurse call her."

Evelyn sat down next to me on the cot. "Why'd you do that, dummy? You could be sick!"

"I'm not sick," I told her. "I just get headaches. My mother has enough of her own without mine, too. Believe me."

"Yeah, I guess she does," Evelyn said. Robert came in and sat down.

"Where's the nurse?" he asked, looking around.

"I don't know, she went out," I said.

"Well, we came to take you home," Evelyn said. "Come on, let's go to your locker and get out of here. Did you take anything?"

"Pills, you mean?" I asked. "No, they're not allowed to give you anything in school. They just give you a cot to writhe on."

"Sounds like a song," Robert said. "*A Cot to Writhe On.*"

Evelyn said, "You're weird, Rose."

∞

They walked me all the way to my corner to make sure I was all right, and then they split before Mom could see Robert. Mom was lying down on the living room couch. That was the usual pattern. When I walked in from the bus stop, that's where she'd be.

"Hi, I'm home," I said loudly.

"Hi," she said, without opening her eyes.

"What'd you do all day?" I asked, knowing the answer. "Did you get the orange juice and rolls?"

"Oh!" She sat up. "Damn! I meant to, honey . . ."

"It's okay," I said. "I'll go. Here's the mail."

"What's in it?"

I looked through the stuff. "Mom?"

"Mm?"

"Here's a bulletin from that group you used to belong to in Lynbrook, remember?"

"Oh. 'Women in the Seventies'?"

"Yeah," I said. "WITS. There's a meeting next Friday night."

"I'm not interested right now . . ."

"Come on. You used to go to all of them," I told her. "Remember? Sunny Robbins' mother went, and Aunt Ruth . . . You even dragged Aunt Lydia once. And she said from that time on, she made Uncle Fred fix his own bologna-and-ketchup sandwiches for the Eleven O'Clock News."

"Oh, Ronnie . . ."

"It says they're going to have a guest lecturer: Dr. Margaret Leslie. She's a psychiatrist, and listen—she's going to talk about 'Single Women As Parents'. Mom?"

"Ronnie, if you're going to the market, will you please go!"

∞

I had begun to give up on Mom and was concentrating on Headache Geraldine when she came into my room a couple of days later.

"Ronnie?"

"What?"

She sat down on the bed, and the extra weight on it made me feel like my body was tilting. I wanted her to get up so I could get level again.

". . . so what do you think?" she said.

"What do I think about what?"

She took a deep breath. "I *said*, this coming Saturday is your birthday and I thought maybe the two of us could do something . . . a little, you know, special."

My birthday. I had forgotten. *Last year what did I do . . . had a party? No, that was when I was twelve . . . Last year we met Daddy in New York and went out for dinner . . .*

"No, I don't want to do anything," I said. *I just want you to get up from this bed,* I thought, *so I can get the two sides of my head together again.*

She didn't get up, she just moved closer to me. "Honey, there must be something . . ."

"Nothing, nothing! I don't want anything, I don't want to do anything!" *And I don't want to cry, so just please go away, go away . . .*

∞

"Ronnie, I have a super idea!" Evelyn said.

We were in the middle of French, the next morning. "It must be Idea Week," I said. "What's yours?"

"Remember back when . . . I mean back before . . . I mean a long time ago I talked to you about maybe going to the opera? You've never been, right?"

"Right."

"Well, this Saturday afternoon they're doing a matinee at the Met. 'La Boheme'! Oh, Ronnie," she bubbled, "that'd be such a great opera for you to see for your first! Let's go get standing room, you, me and Robert!"

"Evelyn, you're bubbling," I said. My eyelids hurt. "Besides, how could Robert go? My mother—"

"Will you stop being such a downer?" Evelyn said. "Honestly, look at your eyes! You look like you could use a whole bottle of Murine. Anyway, your mother doesn't have to know Robert's along. We'll be in New York, after all. What does she do, have you *tailed* or something? Come on! You'd love it—it's so beautiful! I've seen it twice!"

"If you've seen it twice, you know how it comes out. Why do you want to go again?"

Evelyn sighed. "That's just why I want you to come, you poor, culturally-deprived person. I want to introduce you to the finer things in life. You know who's singing? Luciano Pavarotti and Renata Scotto!"

"What does that mean translated?" I asked.

"That does it!" Evelyn said. "You're coming Saturday. You'll love it, I promise."

"Faites attention, mes jeune filles!" Miss Ignelsi sang.

Evelyn waited for Miss Ignelsi to get involved in something else and then she whispered. "What do you say, okay?"

"Saturday's my birthday," I mumbled.

"Perfect!" Evelyn cried and quickly clapped a hand over her mouth as Miss Ignelsi whirled around. " 'Scusez-moi, Mademoiselle," Ev said and smiled weakly. Then she passed me a note that said: *My mother will call your mother and ask if you can go. Now, will you learn to keep your mouth shut in class?*

∞

"I can't," Robert said on the bus home.

"Don't you start, too, Rose," Evelyn said.

"No, kiddo, I really can't go. I have something to do. You and Ronnie go."

"What have you got to do Saturday?" I asked.

"Oh, just . . . nothing too much. I mean, it's *much*, but nothing *too* much. Nothing *special* is what I mean. It's just that I made this commitment, I promised that I'd . . . do this . . . thing."

"Oh," I said.

"Don't believe him," Evelyn said. "He's just jealous of Luciano Pavarotti."

Robert wasn't going to tell me what he was doing and I thought that was kind of funny. Funny-peculiar. It wasn't like him. For a minute I thought he was doing something for my birthday, but then I remembered he couldn't know it was my birthday. Even I had forgotten until Mom reminded me. Evelyn hadn't had a chance to tell him, I was sure, and I hoped she wouldn't.

The phone rang while we were at dinner, which

always annoyed Mom. She never let me answer it then and she always said, "Hel-LO?" Like that, with the accent on the "Lo."

"Yes? Oh, yes. Hi."

It's for her, I thought, *thank God*.

"You mean *this* Saturday?" I heard her say. Okay, it was Mrs. Racanelli, then. I hoped Mom would say yes. I had no headache and the idea had grown on me. I really wanted to go now.

Mom went on talking and I made believe I wasn't paying attention. "She *did?* She told Evelyn that? . . . Oh . . . Well, uh, I guess so. I don't see why not. Thank you . . . Yes, fine thanks. 'Bye."

"That was Evelyn's mother."

"Oh?"

"She said Evelyn wants to take you to the opera this Saturday. She said you told Evelyn you really wanted to go . . ."

"Yeah . . ."

"Does she know it's your birthday? Is that why she asked you?"

I looked up at Mom. "She knows."

"I didn't know you wanted to see an opera," Mom said.

"Evelyn says you don't *see* an opera. You *hear* one," I said.

"I hope you enjoy it," Mom said.

∞

"I don't understand why we have to stand up. Why can't we sit down?" I asked Evelyn.

"Because. Take my word for it. The *real* opera buffs stand. It's the ones who just want to tell their friends that they went to the opera who sit down," she answered.

"I find that hard to believe," I told her. "They're very bright people, who know that the human body was built to bend into a sitting position when it's going to be in one place longer than an hour. Evelyn, look. There are two lines: one for standing places and one for seats. As long as we have a choice . . ."

Evelyn looked at me like a tired teacher. "Ronnie, *look* at the two lines."

"I'm looking."

"Don't you notice a difference?"

"Yeah. The ones buying seats look more intelligent."

"No, Ronnie, the ones in this line are *our* kind of people. They *care* about the music. Look, they even have scores under their arms, some of them. See? When the opera starts, they'll spread the scores out on the floor and follow the opera as it's being performed."

"Which means they'll be sitting down," I persisted. "We don't have any scores so we have to stand. Hey, look! That girl has a score under her arm and she's in the sitting-down line!"

Evelyn looked and sniffed. "Well . . . she's probably going to be 'way up near the ceiling. I guess the students go up there. But it's too high for me. I'll get a bloody nose."

I sighed. "Okay. Tell me about this opera so I know what I'll be seeing. *Hearing*, I mean. All I understand in French is 'Faites attention!' "

"It's not in French, it's in Italian," Evelyn said. "It's about these artists and musicians in Paris in the nineteenth century. The main characters are Rudolfo and Mimi, he's a poet, she has T.B. And they meet and fall in love and part . . ."

"Sounds like a soap opera," I said.

". . . And there are two other main characters, Musetta and Marcello, and *they* fall in love and part . . ."

"EV-e-lyn . . ."

"But the main thing is the beautiful music they sing while they're falling in love and parting. And at the end, Mimi dies and everyone's miserable."

"Happy birthday, Ronnie," I said.

∞

Actually, I liked it. I liked it so much, I even stopped teasing Evelyn and told her so. And I remembered the song—*aria*, I mean—that Diane's mother sang at the variety show, *Mi chiamano Mimi*, which means "My name is Mimi" or "They call me Mimi." But my favorite was *Musetta's Waltz*. I told Evelyn that and she was really happy. She said that was her favorite, too. And both of us cried when Mimi died. Evelyn said I was such a good student that next time she'd take me to Wagner, whatever that means.

Chapter 23

I got some babysitting jobs during the spring. Beverly had told me if I charged seventy-five cents an hour instead of the usual dollar or dollar-and-a-quarter that everyone else charged, I'd get more jobs, and I guess she was right. I had about eighteen dollars saved to pay Mr. Rose.

Robert came over to most of the houses where I sat. Mom never checked and we never got caught. He got there after the kids were asleep, and he managed to be out of the house by the time the people came home, too. Those were nice, fun times. I usually got a headache after each one, but I didn't even care. There was one bad triplet of headaches: Larry, Molly and Norman—three beauts that came right on top of each other—Molly and Norman in the same day—that almost sent me over the edge, but then Headache Patsy didn't come for three days after that. I think it was three days . . . May was a pretty blurry month.

Toward the end of it, I got another job at the Kelseys'. Robert and I loved it there, we went crazy with the bean bag chairs. And besides, their kids were always asleep the whole time. I don't think I'd even recognize Kenny or Frances Kelsey if I ever met them with their eyes open.

That night we were sitting on the chairs watching a Carol Burnett re-run and Robert suddenly rolled his bean bag chair right next to mine, leaned over and took my face in both his hands. Then he kissed me. On the lips. I closed my eyes, and when I opened them, he was holding my hands and smiling at me.

I don't know how long we sat there, looking at each other, but the next thing I knew, the Kelseys were standing there in the kitchen door with my mother.

I found out later that Mom had decided on the spur of the moment to keep me company babysitting, and that she arrived at the same time the Kelseys got home. Robert and I hadn't seen the headlights, hadn't heard the car, hadn't heard the garage door open, hadn't heard anything.

The next hour was Nightmare City. I got hit with such a blinding headache—it had no build to it at all—that I threw up. Right on the bean bag chair, in front of the World. Mrs. Kelsey cleaned me up while Mom cleaned up the bean bag chair, which Mrs. Kelsey kept yelling was naugahyde, not leather so don't worry, which made no sense to me then. I think Robert was standing there the whole time, but I don't really remember because I didn't want to look at him.

When we got home, Mom took my temperature, which was normal, and put me to bed. She didn't say a word.

That was my "R" headache, the stupidest, most awful one of all, so I named it after me: Headache Ronnie, short for nothing.

Mom never said anything about that night and about me being with Robert. I waited and waited but the blowup never came. Only I kept thinking, the way things are with us, we might as well be living in two different universes.

Thank God for Arthur. He was like a messenger from heaven. He was about the only thing that made Mom laugh at all, and even though it wasn't too often, it was something.

He had learned to whistle "Frere Jacques, Frere Jacques, Dormez—" and also, "Twinkle, Twinkle, Little Star; How I—" Sometimes he was off-key, but he always knew it and started all over again till he got it right. He also said "pretty boy" and "spoon-fed." *I* knew it was "spoon-fed" because I taught it to him, but if you didn't know the joke, it sounded like "OOOOh—Ed." I guess it's hard to get the sounds of "S" and "F" when you've only got a beak.

Sometimes when I was having a headache, he would sit on the headboard of my bed and watch me. If a bird can have a worried expression, he did. Just knowing he was worried about me sometimes made me feel better.

A couple of weeks after the Kelsey episode, which was not even mentioned by anyone, including Robert, Evelyn called with another babysitting job for me.

"This is a good one," she said. "The people are going to be out all day and night. There's only one kid and it's a baby, about eight months old. They're great at that age, all they do is eat and sleep."

"How do *you* know?" I asked her.

"Because that's all *I* did," she said.

"That's all you do *now*," I told her.

"Watch it, sister, you're the straight man, remember?" she said. "Listen, you want this job or not?"

"Hold on, I'll check . . ."

I put the phone down and went to find Mom, who was balancing her checkbook in her bedroom.

"I've got a long babysitting job for this weekend," I said. "Afternoon and evening. Okay?"

She didn't even look up. "No more babysitting," she said.

"Huh?"

"I said you won't be babysitting any more."

"I understood the words," I said. "I just don't get it."

"If I can't trust you, and I see that I can't, I'll have to take away the temptation. Robert Rose is off limits," she said, "and so is babysitting."

"But what about the money?" I wailed. "I have

to pay Mr. Rose back for breaking his slides! I only have twenty-one dollars."

"No more babysitting. You can spend that day cleaning out the basement and I'll pay you for it." She went back to the checkbook.

I just stood there, staring at her while she wrote.

"I HATE YOU!" I screamed at her. "I WISH IT WAS YOU THAT DIED INSTEAD OF DADDY!"

Finally I had made her look at me. And when she did, I just ran out of there and into my own room, slamming the door. I lay down on my bed ready to cry. But I didn't. And I didn't get a headache, either.

I also forgot Evelyn on the phone, who had a lot of interesting words for me the next day.

∞

"Have two people ever been so miserable?" Robert asked me in school.

"Oh, sure, I guess so."

"Name two," he said.

"Romeo and Juliet," I said, right off the bat. "And they were our ages, too."

"Look, Ron," he said, "I've got an idea. About how we can go out again and have a date like normal people."

"Are you kidding? There hasn't been one normal thing in our lives since we met!"

"Well," he said, "not normal, exactly, but we can get out. Do you have a small stepladder?"

"Yeah . . . In the garage."

"Well, Friday night, I'll get it, put it under your window, and we'll sneak out. How about it? Hey, it'll be something different to put in your Memory Book."

"Robert," I said, "if there's one thing I don't need, it's another "memory" for my Memory Book. I'm busy *erasing* from my Memory Book!"

"Aw, Ron . . . Do we want to be together or not?"

"Yes, I want to be with you," I said quietly.

I looked at him. He was so good—so dependable, so sweet and funny. *Why did everything have to turn out so badly?* I thought, *I didn't do anything wrong, why am I being tossed around like a rag doll all the time?* I felt so tired . . .

"We'll do it," I said. "I don't even care what happens any more. I've been caught in so many lies one more won't even matter."

"Here's what you do," he said. "About 7:00 or 7:30 go into your room and turn on the radio. Come out a few times, putter around, you know, and finally, about 8:00 just say you're really tired and you're going to rest. But tell your mother you want to leave the radio on, it helps you sleep better, all right?"

"What's the radio for?" I asked.

"To cover any noises we'll make and also to keep her thinking you're really in there. If she thinks you're listening she won't wonder what you're thinking, or what you're doing. It's like in the mystery movies, where they keep the shower running while they're sneaking out. Running water soothes people; they'd never believe you'd walk out on a shower running. *Especially* at a time of conserving our natural resources!"

"Then maybe I should leave the shower running instead of the radio," I told him.

He shook his head. "No . . . it's good, but I think it was only meant to work on TV. Stick with the radio and the ladder."

∞

The escape went pretty smoothly. I turned on a loud rock station, which I don't do *that* often, but sometimes, and told Mom I preferred not to be disturbed. She didn't even answer and I guessed she was just as glad not to have to disturb me.

At exactly 8:00, there was a tap on my window. My room window was on the *side* of the house, so if you were really looking, you could see it from the front, especially at this time of year, when it wasn't quite dark yet. Luckily, we had these weird-looking bushes, right to the left of my window, so Robert was pretty well hidden by them.

There was his face, visible from the nose up, right outside my window. I looked at my desk for a second, because I would have to climb on that to get out the window and when I looked up, his face was gone. I leaped up on the desk, totally panicked, to see what happened, and there he was, lying in the mud, under the ladder. He'd fallen off. I was laughing so hard, I had to race to turn up my radio even louder.

But I did get out. No one bothered me and we brought the ladder around to the back and leaned it against the house.

"Where're we going?" I asked him.

"Casa Loma," he said. "We'll get a pizza. Okay?"

We started to walk.

"Listen, I've got something to tell you," we both said at the exact same time and started to laugh.

"You first," Robert said.

"No, mine's bad news. *You* first."

"Mine's *good* news," he said. *"You* go first. Let's have the bad over with."

"Well . . . I can't babysit anymore. You know, after what happened at the Kelseys'. But I'm cleaning out our basement, and so I'll still be able to earn the money to pay back your father. I only need about nine more dollars . . ."

Robert took my arm and stopped walking. He turned me around to face him.

"You didn't trust me," he said.

"Huh?"

"I told you *I'd* get the money for the slides. I told you I'd never let you pay for them. Didn't you believe me?" I looked at his face. He was really angry.

"Well, but . . . I mean, I just figured it'd be easier for me to do it. The babysitting . . . it was a way for us to be together, but I was earning money at the same time. You knew that . . ."

He let go of my arm. "I wanted you to babysit so we could be together," he said. "But not for the money. How could you think I'd let you . . . Anyway, that's what I wanted to tell you. That was *my* news. That day you and Ev went to the opera? Remember I told you I had something to do?"

"Yeah, I remember. You didn't tell us what," I said.

"I had a playing job. I played piano at an afternoon cocktail party. That was my first. I've had two more since then and I paid my father the thirty dollars. I even have some left. I wanted to surprise you."

"Oh, Robert . . ." I touched his face. He looked so hurt. "I'm sorry. I really didn't think about the money. I mean, it didn't seem to matter which one of us got it . . ."

"It mattered to me," he said.

"I'm sorry," I said again. "I won't not believe you any more. I promise."

By the time we got to the Casa Loma he had taken my hand.

We walked in and looked for a table that couldn't be seen very well by the rest of the people in the restaurant. There was only one and sitting at it were Mr. Vincent and Miss Fisk.

Robert and I looked at each other.

"Should we go over and say hello?" I asked.

"No," he said, "I'm sure they want to be left alone. Let's sit somewhere else."

"Robert . . ."

"What?"

"I want to sit with them," I told him.

"How come?"

"Because . . ." I thought very hard. "Because nobody wants them to be together, either. And because I like them."

Robert said, "You know, my father was mumbling about them last night. He said they ought to be fired. Can you imagine? He doesn't give a damn about anybody but himself, but he has to stick his nose into the business of two people he doesn't even know. He and those biddies in the bridge club . . ."

"Let's sit with them, Robert," I said.

"They don't look happy tonight, Ron," he said.

"That's why. Come on."

We walked over to their table.

"The Dynamic Duo!" Mr. Vincent smiled. "Pull up a chair! In fact, pull up two."

Robert got them and we sat down.

"What's wrong with you two?" Miss Fisk asked. "You look like two longtailed cats in a roomful of rocking chairs."

"We were thinking the same thing about you," I said.

They looked at each other and smiled. "How

about if we treat you to a pizza?" Mr. Vincent asked.

"Oh, wow, we couldn't let you do that. Okay," Robert said and we all laughed.

Mr. Vincent was great. It was hard to get a conversation going right away because there were about a thousand subjects we all wanted to stay away from, but he started talking about movies and music and then we found there were a whole bunch of things we could talk about. Robert told them about his audition for "Name That Song" and they really roared. Robert didn't even spill a thing.

At about 10:00 I decided I had to go back. I just couldn't press my luck any more. As we got up to leave, Miss Fisk pulled me over and gave me a kiss on the cheek. I was embarrassed but it made me feel good. No teacher ever kissed me before.

When we got to my house the ladder was lying in the driveway.

Chapter 24

"Go home, Robert," I said.

"No, I'm not leaving you."

"Go home, GO HOME!" I screamed at him, when the door opened and the outside front lights went on. Mom was standing in the doorway looking at us.

Something exploded in my head. I began to run . . . away from the house, away from my mother, away from Robert . . . My head began to hurt, just a little, but all I could think of while I was running was that I was free, I was finished, it was over. I would never go home again, I would never see anyone I knew . . .

It was the Casa Loma I ran to. I didn't plan on that, but that's where I ended up. I can imagine what I must have looked like because both Miss Fisk and Mr. Vincent were out of their chairs and over to me before I knew what was happening. They brought me to their table and I remember Miss Fisk pushing a glass of water at me but I was so hysterical I just kept sobbing.

Mr. Vincent was repeating, "Is it Robert? Did

something happen to Robert?" but all I could do was shake my head. I could hardly breathe.

"Ronnie, let us take you home," Miss Fisk said gently.

"*NO!*" I screamed, and I saw Miss Fisk turn around to look at the people in the place. "I'm not going home, I'm *NOT* going home!"

"Okay, all right, honey," she said, pulling me close. "Vince, go pay our check. Come on, hurry up."

"Where we going?" he asked quietly, counting out change for a tip.

"My place," she answered. "Let's get her out of here."

∞

Her place was a studio apartment within walking distance of the school.

Mr. Vincent started to come in, too, but Miss Fisk stopped him at the door.

"Girl talk, Vince," she said. "I'll call you tomorrow."

I went into the bathroom, and when I came out, Miss Fisk was boiling water.

"You like tea?" she asked.

I nodded.

"Me, too. But plain ol' Lipton, not any of that exotic stuff," she said.

"I never had any," I said.

After a few minutes, she brought in two mugs of

tea and we sat down together at a little dinette table.

"Honey, I'm going to call your mother—Now, don't get upset . . ."

I was halfway across the room toward the door.

"We can't let her worry all night about where you are. But you can stay here tonight."

I put my hands up to my head. It was getting worse. Headache Thomas.

"I *want* you to stay here tonight, Ronnie, I really do. But let me call, okay?"

"Okay. But I don't want to talk. And I'm not going home," I said. I went back in the bathroom because I didn't want to hear even Miss Fisk's end of the conversation.

When I came out, she was off the phone. I didn't ask her what was said. I just sat back down at the table and sipped my tea.

"It's okay," she said after a minute or two. "You can spend the night here."

"Thanks, Miss Fisk," I said.

"Listen, as long as we're gonna be roommates, why don't you just call me Jane?"

I looked up and smiled.

"But not in Gym," she said. "It wouldn't sit well with the rest of the troops."

"Right," I answered.

"Well? You want to tell me why we're having this cozy little party?"

Nothing from me.

"You don't have to, Ronnie. I'm not trying to pry, honestly. But it might make you feel better if you talk about it."

I couldn't help it, I started to cry.

"Look," she said, picking up my hand, "I'm not a relative, I'm not someone who's known you all your life . . . and honey, I'm certainly not going to pass judgment on you. But I really want to help if I can . . ."

So that's how it came out—the whole story. It came out through some tears and through Head-ache Thomas and through three cups of tea and through three more trips to the bathroom. But she got it all, right from the time we first moved to Uniondale. She only stopped me a couple of times, just to ask a question or something, but she didn't make any remarks about any of it, she just listened to the whole thing. It was almost 1:00 a.m. when I got finished.

Miss Fisk put her elbows up on the table and rested her face on her hands. I did the same, and we sat like that for a long time.

"Tell me something," she said finally. "You think all this is your fault?"

I didn't answer.

"Mama's fault?"

No answer.

"Robert's?"

Nothing. My mind was racing. "Okay, tell me this: when you think about your father, what are your feelings?"

"Why do you ask that?" I said.

"Do you feel a little angry at him?" she asked.

"No! How can you feel angry at someone who's—I don't think about my father," I said.

"It's *all right* to feel anger toward him," she said. "It's *normal*. He's gone. He left. And suddenly your world fell apart. But you think it's not logical to feel angry at him, don't you? The books tell you you're supposed to feel only sorrow."

I nodded.

"They don't tell you about all those so-called bad feelings you get about someone who's died and left you, so you put those out of your mind along with the pain and you just take all that guilt and hurt and lay it somewhere else. Or on someone else."

Headache Thomas was pounding again.

"Everybody does it, Ronnie."

"I don't want to think about that," I said. "I can forget all that when I go out with Robert and I'm with my friends. I can laugh, I can have a good time. She just wants to drag me back down there with *her*."

"Everybody's pain goes in different directions, Ronnie. All of this business wasn't anyone's *fault*. The thing to do now, is figure out how you're going to deal with what comes next."

"I'm not going home," I said.

"Sure you are," she said. "But not like this. You're going to *want* to . . ."

"No!"

". . . Just as much as your mother *wants* you there."

"She's all changed," I said. "She's not the same."

"Of course she's changed," Miss Fisk said. "But she loves you just as much as ever. And now both of you are going to have to work hard at a relationship that just seemed to come easy before. A relationship . . . between two people . . . is never all fun and games, Ronnie. It takes work. And guts."

She wasn't looking at me any more. She was looking at her empty teacup and playing with her spoon.

"Miss . . . uh . . . Jane?"

She smiled. "What?"

"Are you talking about . . . I mean, you—You don't just mean me, do you? I mean, I don't want to pry, either, but . . ." *Boy*, I thought, *why did I open my mouth?* "I mean," I added, "I like you, too."

She put her hand up to my cheek. "Well, I guess the small town grapevine has gotten to you, too, hasn't it?"

"Just a little," I said, looking down.

"Did you hear about the vigilante committee?" she asked.

I nodded.

"Well, they met with the principal to see if Vince and I, or one of us, could be transferred to another school system."

"Oh, no," I groaned.

"I don't think it'll happen, though," she said. "We're certainly going to fight it. We're not hurting anyone and we're not interfering with anyone's lives in the community."

"Yeah, but—"

"Listen, that's my problem. You've got enough of your own. Your mom's coming to get you in the morning, and I think it would be very beneficial if you two were to have a nice long talk, right here on neutral ground. I'll get out of here real early."

"No!" I said. "You stay."

"Okay, okay, don't get upset. I'll stay until it looks like you don't need me any more, how's that?"

"You stay," I said. My headache was gone.

∞

Mom came over at 8:30 the next morning. We were hardly up. Actually, Miss—I mean, Jane—was. She was in a bathrobe and making coffee, but I was still asleep.

Mom kissed me and woke me up.

"Hi, babe," she said. For a second, it was just like I was carried back in time, before anything—any of this—happened. Mom was waking me up for school, like she sometimes used to when I'd

slept through my alarm. Her face was just the same
. . . something about her eyes.

"I missed you," she said.

"Would you like some coffee, Mrs. Rachman?"
Jane asked.

"It's 'Dorothy'," Mom said. "And yes, I would.
Thanks."

"Sure," Jane said and tried to disappear into her
perfectly-open kitchenette.

"Sorry I ran away," I said.

"No," she said, "you're not. I'm sorry you had
to."

Miss Fisk—Jane—brought a cup of coffee and
handed it to Mom, who was still sitting on the edge
of the cot that we'd set up the night before. Then
she went back into the kitchenette.

"Ronnie," Mom began, "I've been so—No, look,
I don't want to go over that again. What matters
now is where we go from here."

I looked for Jane. I wanted to smile at her, I
wanted to say "That's just what you said," but she
was out of view.

"After you ran off last night, Robert came into
the house," Mom said.

"He *did?*"

"It wasn't an easy thing for him to do. Poor kid,
he was scared to death of me."

"I know."

"But he came in, and he told me about the slides.

That you told his father you broke them. That was quite a thing to do, Ronnie."

"Well, what he did was something, too," I said. "To go into the house and tell you that . . . face you, after everything that's happened . . ."

"Those were lovely presents you gave each other," Mom said. "I guess . . . I just misinterpreted your feelings for him, and his for you. I just didn't realize how you needed him. And why."

"He's really a good person, Mom," I said.

"So are you, Ronnie." She stood up. "Get your clothes on, babe. I need you home."

After we left Jane's—I hugged her till I thought she would break in two—Mom and I went home.

Mom talked about pulling herself together, for my sake, she said, but mostly for her own. She said she had stayed up all the night before thinking about how empty the house was without me. She didn't even mention Daddy. She just talked about how much she had missed me. Me!

I talked about Daddy. All the things that stood out in my mind from the time I was little—and when we got to the funny things, we laughed. And Mom didn't make me feel bad for laughing and she didn't look like she felt bad either. And when we got to the accident, we didn't—push it away. Mom told me just what happened: how one minute they were driving along and the next, this strange car just veered over the white line and headed toward them. Mom said she remembered screaming but that it happened so fast—it was over so quickly—

She cried, but so did I. It was okay. This crying was different. I don't know how it was different, but it was. I just know I felt like I lost a hundred pounds.

I was so exhausted by about 4:00 that I had to take a nap. I knew it would be all right for me to call Robert, and I knew I should because he would be worried, but I had to sleep first.

Mom woke me for dinner.

"I have something to tell you," she said. "I hope you like it. I probably should have asked you first, but I wanted it to be a surprise. If you don't like the idea, you don't have to do it."

"What? What?" I said.

"Do you remember Katherine Cope? That college friend of mine who used to visit us in Lynbrook? She's a dancer."

"Kitty? Sure I remember. She tried to give me a lesson once, in the dining room. She said I should take up oil painting, like you." We both laughed. "She moved to California, didn't she?"

"Yup. She's working in television out there and I just called her. How would you like to spend the summer in Los Angeles?"

"You're kidding!"

"I'm not. She'll be delighted to have you. She'll show you a wonderful time."

"But wait a minute—how can we afford that?" I asked.

"We'll use some of the insurance money," she answered. "Your father would have liked that."

"Mom . . . maybe this could be my birthday present. Remember you asked me what I wanted and I said 'nothing'? Well, this'll be it: a late present."

Mom sat down on the bed. "No, dear. That's *not* going to be your present. We'll decide about a present another time. But the trip is not for that reason. You and I haven't communicated very well for a long time, so we might as well end that situation right now. This trip is my way of telling you . . . that I respect you. As a person. I know you're growing up, and growing away from me in one sense, and that that's how it's supposed to be. After your Daddy died, I didn't want to accept that, but I'm ready to now. You need to be independent . . . and I do, too. And then we can be close again. Do you understand?"

"Oh, yes," I said. "I understand."

"And this trip is also to tell you . . . how much I love you."

Chapter 25

There were two more weeks before school let out for summer vacation. I counted every hour. I saw a lot of Robert those two weeks, and Evelyn, too. We had wonderful times—Lenny drove us to the beach on weekends when it was really hot; we went to a carnival where Robert won a really ugly cat for me and I won a really ugly wallet for him; we went to the "Y"—we did a lot. But in the back of my mind was *California*.

If I closed my eyes, I could see C-A-L-I-F-O-R-N-I-A spelled out in different colored letters, with glittery gold around each one. And then the letters all shimmered together to make a rainbow, with guess what at the end of it! Adventure, adventure, adventure was all I could think of.

"Gee, Ron, we could have such a wonderful summer together," Robert said one evening on the beach. "Don't you want to stay home? Do you have to go to California?"

I couldn't explain it to him. I could hardly explain it to me.

"It's not to hurt you," I told him. "But the idea

of getting away—you know, from *everything* for a while—it'll be getting my head together again. You know how it's been for me, Robert. I'm still getting headaches."

He looked puzzled. "You still are?"

"Yeah. Headache Wilma came last night. In the middle of 'The Rockford Files'. Please. Please understand. It isn't you. I just have to have a change of scene."

"I understand," he said, playing with some sand. "I wish I could go with you. Maybe I can hitch out there!"

I threw sand at him.

∞

Three days before my plane was to leave, Evelyn came running over to my house. She pounded on the door until Mom let her in.

"My God, Evelyn, what's wrong?" Mom cried. I came running out of the den.

"What happened?" I said, grabbing her shoulders.

"The most fantastic news!" she gasped. "I just came from Robert's . . . Oh, let me sit down. People my size should never run three whole blocks!" She staggered over to the couch and sank into it, still panting.

"*What?*" I screeched.

But she just held up her hand until she could catch her breath.

I looked up at Mom. "She needs a cupcake or something," I said. "Go get her some food!"

Evelyn grinned, nodded and panted. "Wait till you hear, wait till you hear!"

"Well, will you tell me? Come on," I said, "what did Karen Farber say now?"

"No, no, it's not Karen. Whew! I'm all right now," she said, leaning back.

"Okay, let's have it."

Mom came in with a piece of cheesecake on a plate. Evelyn smiled, thanked her and took it.

I grabbed it. "Oh, no! You're not getting your mouth full until you tell me," I said.

She grabbed it back. "I can't tell you," she said.

"Evelyn Racanelli, you're gonna get this pie in your face if you don't cut it out—"

"No, Ronnie, I mean it, I can't tell you. Robert wants to. He's on his way over, as soon as he gets off the phone with . . . I can't tell you."

"Off the phone with *who?*" I yelled. "Tell me, I can't stand it!"

But she just shook her head. "Nope, he's got to tell you himself." And in went a forkful of cheese-cake.

I went to the door and looked down the block. Robert was running toward our house and every few feet he'd jump in the air and yell "WOW!"

"This better be good . . ." I said to Evelyn.

Robert came charging in, knocking over the umbrella stand.

"I made it!" he screamed, "Ron, I made it! I'm gonna be on 'Name That Song'! They just called a little while ago. I have to be in the city for the taping next Monday. I made it, I-made-it, I-made-it!"

"Oh, Robert!" I screamed back at him. "Oh, Robert, that's incredible!" I grabbed him around the waist and hugged him. Together we jumped around the living room. Evelyn was calm by this time, polishing off the cheesecake.

"Robert, that's just terrific," Mom said. "Your family must be so proud."

Robert let go of me. "Well . . . they don't all know yet. I guess I'll tell my father when he comes home tonight."

"It'll be fine, Robert," Evelyn said.

"Yeah," he said, and suddenly turned to me. "Come with me, Ron."

"Oh, Robert, I can't," I told him. "I'm leaving Sunday."

"Can't you leave sometime next week?" he begged. "It won't be the same without you."

"It's all you, Robert," I said. "It's not me. You'll do great, no matter who's there. You know I'll be thinking of you all the time." I took his hand. "I will, Robert. And I'll call you Monday night. From L.A." Mom tilted her head at me. "I mean, with my own money," I said. "I've got this twenty-one dollars hanging around . . ."

∞

I spent Saturday with Robert alone. We didn't do anything. I had some last-minute packing to do and he "helped" by spilling grape juice on my denim skirt while he was folding it up.

I packed my picture of "Little Sad Sack" and it made Robert smile.

"What about Arthur?" he asked.

"Oh, I'm taking him," I said. "I'm going to carry him in a little box with holes in it. His cage can go in baggage."

"I don't think they'll let you, Ron," Robert said. "They make all the pets ride in the pet compartment."

"No way is Arthur riding in the pet compartment with a bunch of dogs and cats."

"Hey, Ron?"

"What?"

He closed one of my suitcases and put it on the floor. "Can I keep him for you? Over the summer? I'll take good care of him, I'll teach him lots of new words. Boy, will you be surprised when you get home!"

"Yeah, I'll bet," I said. "That's really sweet, Robert. But what about your father?"

"Arthur'll be in my room. He won't even see him. I know it'll be okay. My mother will calm the old man down."

"No, he might hurt him," I said.

"He won't. Look, I'll tell you what, if it doesn't

work out, I'll bring him home. Your mother will take care of him. But you can't take him with you in the passenger part of the plane. He'd be much better off here . . . Besides," he went on, "my father's been different since he found out about my going on the show. I kept telling him about the money I could win, and what really turned him around was when I told him I'd try for the car."

"The car? That's the jackpot!" I said.

"Don't you think I can win the jackpot?" he asked, hurt.

"Of course I do," I said. I reached into the zippered compartment of my overnight bag. "Here," I said, handing him an envelope. "Take this with you for luck."

"What is it?" he asked.

"It's a picture of a very unusual young man and his special friend."

I got another kiss. On the lips.

∞

My plane was leaving from Kennedy Airport at 9:30 the next morning, so Mom and I had to leave the house at 7:30, just to be on the safe side— avoiding traffic, getting checked in, and all that. Robert and I arranged to meet on the corner of my street, Walnut, and Railroad Avenue at 6:00 a.m. to say a last goodbye.

I could have sworn I set my alarm. I did set it, because when I looked at the hand, it was pointing at 5:30. But either I turned it off without even waking up or I had forgotten to pull out the alarm button. Anyway, I didn't make it, I woke up at 6:45, when Mom came into my room. I felt so bad—I would have called, except it was so early on a Sunday morning—his father would have had a fit. Mom promised to call him later and explain, and also to check about whether he could keep Arthur or not.

I gave Arthur a kiss on the beak and he said "Awk," which I guess was short for "awkward."

I got my last headache in the car, but it wasn't a bad one. And Mom made me feel so good at the airport, fussing over me and buying me magazines and stuff, that it only lasted till Omaha.

Together and
Apart

Chapter 26

"Ronnie! Ronnie Rachman!"

I was carrying my overnight bag and the magazines Mom had gotten me and it was hard to turn my head. The voice was coming from somewhere over my right shoulder.

"Here, give me the bag! Hi, hon!"

Now I was able to turn. "Kitty?" I asked.

"Sure! Didn't you recognize me?"

I smiled at her. "I just didn't *see* you. Of course I recognize you. You haven't changed a bit!"

She grinned back. "Neither have you," she said, "except you've grown up."

∞

On Monday morning, Kitty took me to a rehearsal for a television show she was choreographing. She was in charge of all the dancing for the whole show. I couldn't believe how they did it. She took all the dancers into a rehearsal studio which was located above the TV stage where they would perform. And then she taught them all the steps *without any music*. Kitty said they learned the dances by counting beats. She said they didn't even need the music, as long as they could count. Afterward, they moved down to the stage, but still had no music. It was weird seeing all these dancers move around to no sound.

We got back to Kitty's little house in the valley at around 8:00, after stopping for a bite to eat. I couldn't wait to call Robert; it seemed like such a long time since I'd seen him, and I wanted to apologize. Oh, and I had so much to tell him.

"Hey, before you call . . ." I heard Kitty yell as I was heading for the phone. "There's a letter here for you . . . and it's from that guy you'll be talking to in a minute . . . Robert Ro-"

"Oh, give it to me!" I cried, grabbing it from her as she laughed and walked into the kitchen. The letter had been written the Thursday before I left. He must have gotten Kitty's address from Mom.

Dear Ron—

I don't have much to report since I just saw you, but I wanted you to be sure to remember me now that you're far away. So I want to welcome you to Los Angeles from Chestnut Street in Uniondale, Long Island.

You can bet I'm missing you a lot right now.

Love,
Robert

I couldn't wait to call him after that. My hand was shaking as I dialed. I heard the operator say, "I have a person-to-person call for Robert Rose," and then Caroline's voice came on the line.

"I'm sorry, operator, he's not here."

Not there?

"Where is he?" I said into the phone. "When will he be back?"

"Would you talk to this party?" the operator asked me.

"Well, no, but—when will he be back?"

"He's not home yet from—" Caroline started to say but we were cut off by the operator.

Kitty said it would be 11:00 in New York. *Where is he at 11:00 at night?* I thought. *Maybe I should have talked to Caroline.*

∞

The next two days were really busy and exciting. I watched Kitty work with the director of the TV show and with the costumer and the arranger, and then I saw how she marked out all her dance steps with the orchestra—finally an orchestra, but no dancers, just Kitty—and then they recorded all the music. And Kitty took me around the studio and showed me some sets for some big TV shows and pointed out some stars. I told her I wouldn't mind wandering around by myself if she were busy. I said not to worry about me, I could take care of myself. She answered, fine, we could do lots of neat things, together and apart. Just what I wanted.

Ronnie and Rosey

Dear Ron—

It's after midnight and I just got back from New York. I'm really sorry I missed your call, but we were out celebrating. Two things you will not believe: One, I was out celebrating with MY FATHER (yes, you're reading right) and two, we were celebrating because I WON THE JACKPOT, I WON THE CAR! A bright red Sting Ray, a two-seater! Guess what the song was? I picked it after listening to just seven notes. I Get Along Without You Very Well. I thought it was funny that that should be my lucky song, since the title sure isn't true for me.

Now pick yourself up off the floor and get this: My father was so excited, he took me out for dinner, and promised to buy the whole family tickets for a Broadway show.

I never saw him like this, Ron, it's really weird. Of course, I'm going to give the car to him, but he says in two more years, when I'm old enough, he'll buy me a car of my own.

I'll let you know when the show is going to be aired, they didn't tell us today.

I miss you more than you know.

Love,
Robert

Hi, Ronnie—

Guess you probably heard from Robert, the Car Magnate. His head is so big, he can't get through the door. We *think he's teed because the town didn't give him a ticker-tape parade. It's very boring. No, it's really terrific.*

Heading out for the beach today with Bev. I'm wearing a tent sundress as usual, but this time, I put a bathing suit underneath. If the beach isn't crowded, maybe I'll even take off the sundress.

You know I won't. Have fun out there.

Love,
Ev

Dear Mom,

It's glorious out here, I am having a perfect time. Kitty is so nice and I am trying to be a good guest. I unpacked all my stuff the first day—ha ha.

Kitty took me on the Universal Studio tours and I saw Lucille Ball's dressing room and a stunt show and a make-up show. Fantastic!

I wrote to Robert. I guess you heard he won the jackpot on "Name That Song." Please call him up for me and tell him I send him a kiss and a hug. I knew he could do it. Thanks for writing me that Arthur is at Robert's. I'm glad it worked out, but I would really appreciate it if you would check on him once in a while and make sure Robert hasn't spilled his birdseed all over everything.

The Robbins' barbecue sounded nice. I'm glad you had a good time. I hope Sunny is having fun at camp.

Miss you.

Love,
Ronnie

Dear ~~Miss~~ ~~Ms~~. Jane

California is beautiful. I spent two days at Disneyland—I really loved it!

Kitty says she will take me to get my ears pierced just like yours and will buy me 'California earrings', whatever they are. I'll bring you back a pair.

I know you will win your fight to stay in our school system.

I think of you all the time.

> *Love,*
> *Ronnie*

Two weeks. That's all I'd been there and I felt like a new person.

Kitty took me to the Farmers' Market. Mainly, it's for fruits and vegetables, but you can buy practically anything in the stalls they have lined up, and the neatest thing is you can watch them decorating cakes. All kinds of cakes, really fancy, with whipped cream and flowers, and all kinds of different colored decorations. And you can eat there, too. I had pastrami and Kitty had corned beef. We met a friend of hers there, Gideon Morgan. He's an actor. Evelyn would love him, he looks just like his name. Anyway, he said his daughter was living with him, he's divorced, and she was about my age. He and Kitty thought it would be nice if we could get together. I hoped we could.

∝

Dear Ronnie,

I haven't heard from you all week, you must really be busy.

I wrote a song for you the other day. It's called "Straight Man." I even wrote the lyrics. Listen, I'm humming it, can you hear it?

I've been to the beach a lot and have a golden tan to show off to you when you come home. It seems like forever.

Arthur is doing just great. Guess who likes him? Harlan! You wouldn't recognize the old man—Ever since they delivered the car (last Tuesday) he's behaving like a kid. My mother walks around the house with her fingers crossed all the time. Looks cute, but she can't get meals cooked very easily.

Please write—

Love,
Robert

Dear Robert—

I'm really glad everything is so terrific with your family.

California is like a dream world. I met this actor's daughter, Mariette (can you believe that?) Morgan. She's thirteen going on forty-five. Ul-tra sophisticated—just like us. Anyway, she took me to Olivera Street. Have you heard of it? It's got all Mexican shops and stalls, the most colorful place I've ever seen. They have mariachi bands playing—all brass, no piano, and you can buy all kinds of gorgeous Mexican stuff. Mariette bought an outfit: Mexican skirt, peasant blouse, silver bracelet. When she bought these fantastic hoop earrings, I couldn't stand it, so she took me to get my ears pierced. I'm writing Evelyn it didn't hurt.

With your golden tan and my new Mexican look, we'll be terrific!

Learn to play the bongos.

> *Love,*
> *Ronnie*

Dear Ev—

Had to write because I just got back from seeing Grauman's Chinese Theater with Kitty and Mariette Morgan and her father. You'd die—you can touch every star's footprints and handprints and—other—prints. They really rolled their bodies all around the sidewalk here.

I also saw Carol Burnett in the beauty parlor. She's even prettier in person than on TV. Kitty was having her hair done because she's performing tonight at this English-type music hall. I'm going to watch.

Boy, is this summer something else!

> *Love,*
> *Ronnie*

Dear Ronnie—

Will you please write to Robert? He's in such a funk I can't stand it. He says he writes you four letters to every one he gets from you. I'm getting worried about the old boy, don't tell him I said so.

Love,

Ev

P.S. Took off my tent dress on the beach the other day! Don't get excited—no one was there—it was raining.

Dear Ron—

Sit down, because I have a long sad story to pour out to you. Please take the time to hear it—It's been so long since I've heard from you I can't tell where your head is right now.

But I have to tell you what old Rosey did. Two nights ago, I was so depressed, I went down to Blue Dell's. They open nights in the summer. I was looking for Sheldon. I wanted to buy some grass from him. I never tried it before, and that's the truth, but I was just feeling so crummy, I thought I'd like to see what it was like to get high. Besides, you know what they say about musicians.

Well, anyway, Sheldon was there with two of his buddies, you know, Harve and Rich? I told Sheldon what I wanted and he and Harve and Rich went into this huddle and pretty soon they came back with two joints they said they'd sell me for five bucks. Sheldon said he was giving me a break because I was his buddy.

Well, babe, I was never a buddy of Sheldon's and I should have suspected something, but I didn't. I took the two joints and went back to Uniondale on the bus, went over to the park, sat on the swings and got ready to swing!

The first joint made me choke worse than that cigarette you saw me smoke a hundred years ago, but I did just what Sheldon said, you know, inhale really deeply and keep it in your lungs and all that. Probably the worst tasting stuff I ever had.

To make a long story short, I got high. I really did. I was feeling terrific and yelling awful things at you, I'm sorry, Ron. I was yelling STAY THERE, STAY IN CALIFORNIA FOR ALL I CARE, WHO NEEDS YOU!

But I do, Ron, I do need you.

Well, anyway, to make a long/short story even shorter, when I got home, Caroline was the only one there and she could see I was definitely not myself and asked me what I was on. I was so stoned I told her. She asked me if I had any left, I said yes, and told her to share it with me. She looked at it, took one sniff and guess what? Oregano.

No dope. Just oregano. Sheldon's little "King Kong" Revenge. Five bucks for a phony high and a paper full of herbs.

Figures, doesn't it?

Write me a letter . . . Tell me how you really are . . . I'm glad you got your ears pierced, now how about your feelings?

> *All my love,*
> *Robert*

Dear Robert,

I'm sorry. I'm sorry about not writing, sorry about the Great Oregano Rip-Off, sorry that you wanted it in the first place.

I told you how badly I needed to be here. I did. Everything at home was such a downer that I needed to get away and forget. I told you that.

I didn't mean you were a downer.

You were the one bright spot and the only thing I had to hold on to.

Let me see if I can explain it.

Okay. Picture this balloon. It's a big one and it looks like it could hold a lot of air, right? And somebody's blowing it up and blowing it up, until it's really enormous. And you're sure *it won't hold another breath of air. But somehow it does, and it does, and it does until suddenly, whoever's blowing it up lets go of it. Just like that. And SWOOSH, it goes flying around the room like crazy until all that air is out of it. All the air. And then it just falls to the floor and lies there.*

Just lies there.

If a balloon had feelings, I know what they would be. The pressure starts inside your head. Only a little at first, so you don't really feel it. Then it comes on a little stronger, and it builds. And it builds and it builds and it builds until you either explode or you let go. Maybe I did both.

The difference is, it takes a minute to blow up a balloon. With me, it took about eight months.

Ronnie and Rosey

    It wasn't you I was trying to forget. It was the whole situation.
    Don't be mad at me please. I love you. I always will.
    Love,
    Ronnie

Chapter 27

The time flew. If the past winter was a blur, the summer was even blurrier, but what a difference. Mom flew out the last two weeks and joined us. And she brought me a birthday present: a small canvas that she had painted with the acrylics I had given her for Christmas. It was a portrait of Arthur!

"It's beautiful!" I cried. "How did you get him to pose for you?"

"He didn't," Mom replied. "Robert has him, remember? I did it from memory."

"Well, it's great," I said. "It has his perfect nasty expression. I love it. Was this the first time you used the acrylics?"

"Yes, but not the last. I really like the texture. I've done quite a few things—you'll see when you get home."

Kitty and Mom were like two little kids. They talked about their college days, they sang songs and danced around Kitty's living room—it was a gas! Mom was just like she used to be, kidding and playing and joking. We went to bed at 1:00 in the morning and slept till noon. Kitty had a party for Mom when she came and she was just in heaven, talking to the dancers and actors about their work—she even brought her sketch book and sketched the valley around Kitty's little house. She even drew me.

And we talked about Daddy. Kitty wanted to know all about him and it was easy talk. Easier even than it had been between Mom and me before I left. The love was there but the hate was gone.

When the summer was over, when it was finally time to go home, I wasn't even sorry. It was like I had been dying of thirst and someone gave me all the water I needed to drink. And my strength came back, and all my energy, and I was okay again.

Kitty saw us off at the plane and helped us carry two Mexican sombreros and a set of bongos for Robert. I had brought a huge flowing Mexican blouse for Evelyn and some Mexican jumping beans for the Kelsey kids. And a pair of big silver earrings for Jane.

"Uniondale Junior and Senior High School is ready to roll, babe," Mom said on the plane. "The way we cut things, you'll probably have to get off the plane, grab your books and head for class."

"You mean school's starting this early?" I asked.

" 'Fraid so. Labor Day's this weekend, and then that's it."

"Mom? Will Jane and Mr. Vincent be back at

the old school? That committee didn't get them out, did they?"

"Well," she said with a smile, "there was another committee. A counter-committee, fighting to keep them on. It wasn't too big a fight. They're both good teachers. They'll stay."

"Oh, wow," I said, "that's a relief!" I looked at her. Something made me ask, "Who was on the counter-committee?"

"To be perfectly honest, it was the chairperson who did most of the work. She made two terrific speeches at a couple of school board meetings. Practically wrung tears out of the old boys."

"The chairperson, huh? Who was it?"

"Wonderful woman. You should get to know her. Dorothy Rachman. Talented, too! Understand she paints . . ."

"Oh, Ma!"

∞

Robert, Evelyn and Caroline were at the airport to meet us. Mom knew they would be there but kept it as a surprise for me. And when we got to the car, there was another surprise: a talking box.

"Pretty, pretty!" said the box. "Won a car! Won a car!"

"Arthur!" I yelled. I opened the box.

"Awk," said Arthur.

"No, baby," I told him. "It's not awkward. It's terrific!"

"Did you hear that?" Evelyn said. "The damn bird walks around yelling 'Won a car, won a car!' Good thing you came back when you did, Ronnie. Robert was grooming the bird to be his agent!"

"Ronnie, tell me about California," Caroline said, as she drove.

"No!" Robert yelled. "I promise not to describe the red leather upholstery in that gorgeous Sting Ray, if Ronnie promises not to take us step by step through Disneyland."

"I promise," I laughed. "But wait'll you see my home movies!"

Everybody groaned.

When we got to good old Walnut Street, Robert helped bring our bags into the house while Evelyn and Caroline waited in the car and Mom thanked them.

"Tonight, Ron? No, guess it's too soon. How about tomorrow?"

"Robert, I just got home . . ."

"Monday? Labor Day?"

I kissed him on the cheek. "Let's wait until school starts Wednesday, okay? Let's see what happens."

He nodded. "Right. Okay. But I won't promise not to call . . . Your mother won't mind."

"No, she won't."

"Look, I brought the cage back. You can put Arthur right in."

"Robert?"

"What?"

"How did that bird live all summer?"

"What do you mean?" he asked, shocked.

"The water and food dishes are upside down."

"Oh, hell," he said. "It wasn't like that all summer. I just threw them in when I put the cage together. You examine him. He's fat as a quail. Evelyn's been feeding him linguini for two months. He thrives on it."

"See you Wednesday," I said. "And thanks for everything."

"Oh, you're welcome," he said and backed out, knocking over the umbrella stand.

After they left, I looked around the house, walking slowly from room to room.

"Mom?" I called from her bedroom.

"Hm?"

"The house is different."

"What?" she asked, coming in.

"I said the house is different. It *feels* different. Is it because both of us have changed so much? I don't know . . ." I waved my arm. ". . . Just isn't the same."

" 'Course it's not the same. I unpacked everything," Mom said.

I looked at her and started to laugh. *"That's* it!" I said. "That's what's different . . . no boxes and cartons. It's like a home now."

"Darn right," Mom said. "How about some Kentucky Fried Chicken?"

∞

How strange. To be able to walk to school after waiting for a bus for so long.

And it was beautiful. The grounds needed work, but the building was gorgeous. All low and new, with lots of glass overlooking fields of—dirt—that would be grass and gardens next spring. The walls were yellow and bright and the blackboards were green. And the rooms smelled new. Clean. Everything was new. It was wonderful.

Actually, that first morning, I didn't walk. I overslept so Mom had to drive me. I was still on California time, I guess.

Ninth grade . . . Getting to know a new building again, but without all the nervousness. Headaches had been a thing of the past since California.

I looked at my schedule card: First period— Math, Room 9-A. Did "A" mean first floor? *No, wait a minute, this whole school is on one floor. Now where am I?*

Crash!

Something hit my back and I was jerked forward. Two looseleafs went flying out of my arms.

"Oh, wow, I'm so sorry," said a voice behind me, and I started to laugh. I laughed until I had to sit down on the floor and lean against a locker.

"I'm really sorry—" the soft voice went on . . .

"Forget it," I said, still laughing. "Just go get my blue book. Some kid is skating down the hall on it."

He did and put it on my lap.

"Hey," I said. "Did you do that on purpose?"

"On purpose?" Robert said, looking hurt. "On purpose? Are you kidding? Would I do that?"

"The truth," I said, holding up my fist.

"Jeez, you lazy students," he said. "You want all your answers spoon-fed!"

Also by Judie Angell
IN SUMMERTIME IT'S TUFFY